THE JETSETTERS

Praise for David-Matthew Barnes

Accidents Never Happen

"Barnes crafts a complex, imaginative, character-driven suspense/romance novel with realistic, gritty people and situations, which make the book a definite page-turner and a must-read for those who appreciate such originality. Though the characters have significant negative experiences, the overall tone celebrates the ability of people to cope and rebound from past setbacks. Five stars."—*Echo Magazine*

"*Accidents Never Happen* makes a perfect summer read as it keeps you guessing and ends with several astonishing twists."—*EDGE*

Swimming to Chicago

"I love books that can destroy their own labels…David-Matthew Barnes' marvelous *Swimming to Chicago* will doubtless be put on the YA shelf…a well-told tale…that will engross readers of all ages…riveting…"—*Out in Print*

"With what has been happening with our gay youth, David-Matthew Barnes gives us a book that is so important…It is not often that I come upon a book that pulls me in so completely… it could be a combination of wonderfully drawn characters, a terrific plot and great writing. Barnes gives us three terrific characters in Alex, Robby and Jillian…I found myself cheering our heroes on and wanting to take them by the hands and lead them through."—*Reviews by Amos Lassen*

"The author's knack for dialogue is indicative of his experience as a playwright. Conversations are honest, gritty, and profound, and most importantly, germane to the story and its outcome."—*EDGE*

Mesmerized

"Barnes' young adult novel about two boys suddenly, deeply in love has a fairy-tale tone, but it will strike all the right notes for YA readers as the boys dance into the hearts of The Showdown audience."—Richard Labonté, *BookMarks*

"There is a wonderful resounding theme: sometimes you have to be brave enough to love and forgive. You won't grasp these words completely unless you read this entire heartrending story…"—*QMO (Queer Magazine Online)*

"…relevant to the plight of many gay teens…a vivid and realistic telling of the emotions and unfortunate realities that can face a teenager in reconciling his sexuality…very well written…four stars…"—*Echo Magazine*

"…a timely work that will resonate with readers for its portrayal of society's perception of the GLBT community…" —*Out & About*

"…a teenage love story, but it's between Brodie and Lance… it explores grief and loss—particularly the difference between having a loved one murdered and choosing to reject someone for being gay."—*Sacramento News & Review*

By the Author

Liberty Editions

Accidents Never Happen

The Jetsetters

Young Adult Fiction

Swimming to Chicago

Mesmerized

THE JETSETTERS

by

David-Matthew Barnes

A Division of Bold Strokes Books

2012

THE JETSETTERS

ISBN 13: 978-1-60282-745-5

This Trade Paperback Original Is Published By
Bold Strokes Books, Inc.
P.O. Box 249
Valley Falls, NY 12185

First Edition: September 2012

Credits
Editors: Greg Herren and Stacia Seaman
Production Design: Stacia Seaman
Cover Design by Sheri (graphicartist2020@hotmail.com)

Acknowledgments

Many people helped bring *The Jetsetters* to print. To them, I offer my deepest gratitude:

To Len Barot, for her unconditional support, shared wisdom, and never-ending faith in my stories.

To Greg Herren, for being a genius editor, a patient teacher, and a brilliant writer.

To the wonderful Bold Strokes Books family, especially Cindy Cresap, Connie Ward, Kim Baldwin, Lori Anderson, Ruth Sternglantz, Sandy Lowe, Sheri, and Stacia Seaman.

To Terri Nunn and the members of Berlin, Dale Bozzio and the members of Missing Persons, Johnette Napolitano and the members of Concrete Blonde, Chantal Claret and the members of Morningwood, Joan Jett and the Blackhearts, The Dollyrots, Voice of the Beehive, and Possum Dixon for providing the perfect soundtrack to this novel, without even realizing it.

For their never-ending support and words of encouragement: Albert Magaña, Amelia Paz, Andrea Patten, Bethany Hidden-Cauley, Billie Parish, Blithe Raines, Bryan Northup, Carmel Comendador, Carsen Taite, Cathy Moreno, Christian Thomas, Collin Kelley, Cyndi Lopez, Danielle Downs, Dawn Hartman Towle, Debbie Otto, Debra Garnes, Dellina Moreno, Donna Cummings, Elizabeth Warren, Frankie Hernandez, Hannah Grimes, Jacqui Kriz, Jamie Hughes, Janet Milstein, January Cummings, Jessica Lopez Murray, Jessica Moreno, Jill McMahon, Jodi Blue, Joyce Luzader, Julie Bloemeke, Karen Head, Karen Vega, Kelly Kinghorn Hurtado, Kelly Wilson Lopez, Kerry Crawford, Keshia Whitmore-Govers, Kimberly Greenberg, Lety Cruz, Linda Wread-Barnes, Linnea Lindh, Lisa

Allender, Logan Hindle, Lynda Sandoval, Marcia Gonzales, Maire Gardner, Marilyn Montague, Marisa Villegas, Melita Ann Sagar, Megan Quinn, Michelle Boman Harris, Mindy Morgan, Nance Haxton, Nea Herriott, Nick A. Moreno, Nita Manley, Patricia Abbott-Dinsmore, Raquel Short, Rena Mason, Robyn Colburn, Sabra Rahel, Sal Meza, Sami McNeil, Selena Ambush, Sheryl Hoover, Stacy Scranton, Stefani Deoul, Stephanie Gomez, Susan Madden, Tara Henry, Teresa Michelle Ruiz, Therease Logan, Trish DeBaun, Todd Wylie, and Vanessa Menendez.

To my wonderful colleagues for putting up with me, particularly Alexis Jackson, Ashley Calhoun Stout, Brad Jester, Christi Ellington, Dawn Hodges, Diane Bertschin, Gail Daniel, Jean Cash, Jennifer Edwards, Kate Williams, Kathlyn Burden, Kelly Batchelder, Leila Wells Rogers, Liz Jester, Lynn Futral, Rebecca Johnson, Shellie Morgan, Sherry Brooks, Sloan Passmore, Teresa Brooks, and Trevor Alexander.

To my parents, Samuel Barnes, Jr. and Nancy Nickle, and my brothers, Jamin, Jason, Andy, and Jaren, for letting me be the writer in the family.

To my students, who teach me more on a daily basis than I could ever dream of teaching them.

To the loving memory of my grandmother, Dorothy Helen Nickle, for my childhood of soap operas and tea parties.

To Edward C. Ortiz, for the wonderful life and love we share.

To the beautiful city of Chicago. And the always-inspiring people who live there.

To God, for everything. Without You, I'm nothing.

And, finally, to Celso Chavez for being the greatest guitar player who ever lived and for always dedicating a song to me. I still can't believe you're gone.

For Edward C. Ortiz,
for not only sharing his love of music with me,
but his beautiful heart as well.

To Edward C. Ott,
for not only sharing the love of music with me
but the beautiful heart as well.

"...you are the music while the music lasts."
—from *The Dry Salvages* by T.S. Eliot

CHAPTER ONE

Since the morning I left Diego Delgado asleep in a hotel room in New York and disappeared from his life forever, I'd been living on the fine line between a broken heart and a nervous breakdown. It was a shitty place to exist, but it was a self-imposed exile. I walked away from love twelve years ago and only had myself to blame for the stupidest choice ever made by a human being. This pissed me off more than anything.

I wasn't bitter, but I drank a lot.

I ordered a second pomegranate martini because the first one hadn't done the trick. The loneliness plaguing me for most of my adult life seemed particularly potent as I sat in a low-lit airport bar at LAX. I lifted the glass, brought the edge of it to my mouth, and tilted my head back. The cool liquid swam down my throat, but the cheap gin couldn't burn away the impending need to cry.

Don't have a meltdown here. Everyone will know you're insane. Suck it up, you crybaby.

I glanced over to the computer bag sitting on the empty bar stool beside me.

You've got work to do. Focus on your job, dumbass. It's all you have left in this world.

For the last twelve years of my life, I'd done just that: I'd lived for my career. As a result, I was a senior copywriter at a successful advertising firm. I owned a lake-view condo in Chicago. I lived with a fat cat named King Louie, who tolerated me at best. I had a circle of sympathetic friends who filled my empty single life with a constant flow of invitations for drinks and dinners. I even knew a few guys who were good for the occasional blow job whenever the need struck—and it rarely did.

Yet I'd never felt more alone in the world.

And to make matters worse, my martini glass was empty.

"Another one?" offered the blond bartender with the body of a Swedish god.

I sighed and shrugged, shifted uncomfortably on the bar stool. I was no good at flirting. Every time I made an attempt, I felt more and more ridiculous. I was convinced I was a freak of gay nature. "Not sure if I should," I said, knowing damn well I was having another drink. "I have a connecting flight to catch."

The bartender leaned in. His sticky, sweet breath smelled like peppermint. He was wearing a tight-fitting white polo and black jeans. "How long is your layover?" he asked in a secretive whisper. *Are we plotting a takeover of the world or working out the details of a drug deal?* I wondered why my martini-serving Adonis was trying to keep our conversation so *hush-hush*. The bar was practically a ghost town.

Then it dawned on me.

Maybe he was incredibly horny and I was a last resort.

And maybe I was better than nothing.

I cracked a smile and tried to avoid staring at the Swede's perfect teeth. Guys like the hot bartender never seemed to notice me. I usually attracted men twice his age and twice my weight. "Five hours," I answered, continuing to grin. "It's ridiculous."

The bartender swiped the empty glass and said, "I'm off in an hour."

I watched, almost mesmerized, as he whipped up another martini. I liked the way his thick fingers held the bottle of gin with confidence and authority. "I appreciate the offer," I said, "and believe me, I could use the company…but…"

A third martini suddenly appeared in front of me. "But you're seeing someone," the bartender finished. "No big deal with me if you are."

I reached for the glass, shook my head. "No. I'm not seeing someone."

"Are you kidding?" The blonde's eyebrows shot up. "A guy like *you*?"

I lowered my glass, licked my lips. I knew they were my best feature—or so I'd been told. "A guy like *me*?"

The bartender leaned in again. This time, his mouth was close enough to kiss. "This is L.A.," he said, as if reminding me where I was. Did I look *that* lost? "I'm sure you must know someone you could spend an hour with."

I held his gaze. "I don't know anyone."

The eyebrows moved again. "You sure about that?"

The bartender turned away but my words stopped him, brought him back. "I mean, I do." I took a breath, a silent leap of faith. "My name's Justin...Justin Holt."

The perfect teeth shone at me again when he flashed an all-too-eager smile. He thought I was a done deal, a sure thing, a slam dunk.

When in the hell did I become so easy?

"Well, Justin Holt, it might be fun to kill some time together," he said.

I nodded and tried my best to act nonchalant. I didn't want to appear desperate. I placed some cash on the bar to pay for my drinks. "Yeah...sure."

He stepped back a little as if he wanted to get a better look at me. Maybe the lighting had changed in the bar and my flaws were now apparent. Maybe he now saw me for the terminally single social pariah I really was. "You seem uptight," he assessed.

I tried to care. "Do I?"

The bartender moved to the register to make change. "Tense, maybe."

I thought about it for a moment, then decided: "No."

"No?"

I lifted my glass again. "No. I'm not tense. I don't have a stressful life. I think…I think I'm just really, really sad." I sniffed to hold my tears back.

The bartender folded his arms across his chest and his biceps flexed naturally. "Anything I can do to cheer you up?"

I nearly laughed. "Probably…at least for a little while. But tomorrow…"

The word *tomorrow* seemed to trigger a silent alarm in his head. A high degree of panic flashed across the bartender's face. "Tomorrow?" he repeated, maybe concerned I was anticipating a marriage proposal by midnight. "I thought you had a plane to catch."

My smile and mood vanished. I could hear the tears in my own voice when I confessed, "Tomorrow is my birthday."

Relief washed over the bartender and his shoulders relaxed a little. "Oh…well…then we should definitely celebrate." He winked this time and the gesture seemed corny.

What a condescending asshole.

"They don't call it a layover for nothing." He smirked.

I pushed the martini glass away.

Music suddenly caught my attention. It was filtered, as if it were seeping out of a pair of ear buds. I turned to my computer bag, worried I'd left my iPod on. Then I realized where the music was coming from.

She was probably no older than twenty-one. She sat farther down the bar, near the flow of frantic and dazed passengers rushing or sauntering past the bar's entrance, from gate to gate. She was an alluring woman, curvy and confident. Her hair was a mess of jagged strands of jet black, hot magenta, and baby blue. A few tattoos poked out of the sleeves and low neckline of the peasant blouse she wore. A rhinestone choker sparkled around her neck and caught the reflection of the low lights in the bar. Her ensemble was completed with a shiny black miniskirt, fishnet tights, and double-knotted combat boots. She looked like a rock star. She looked a lot like Halo Jet. But I knew she wasn't Halo. That was impossible.

She bobbed her head to the drum-heavy rhythm of the song blasting in her ears. She moved her mouth to the lyrics; the words were an extension of her tortured soul. I wasn't only enraptured with this woman, I was thankful to her. She was the sign I'd been waiting for, a reminder of my past and its incompleteness.

I recognized the song immediately. After all, it'd been written about me twelve years ago. Me, before the corporate career, before the predictable condo life, before the lame-ass twisted form of self-punishment I'd subjected myself to all these years.

I struggled with the impulse to speak to the woman, to tell her about the immediate connection I felt with her.

I once knew someone a lot like you.

She looked at me. I wondered if she sensed what I was feeling.

No, that's not an empathetic expression on her face. She's deeply annoyed by my presence. She wants me to leave her alone and mind my own fucking business.

Stop looking at her, you idiot. Look away, damn it!

She tugged the white ear buds away from her face and shot me a death stare. "Don't tell me," she said in a voice permanently drenched with tequila. "The music is too loud and it's bothering you."

I shifted on the bar stool to face her. "On the contrary," I said.

She glanced me over. Clearly, I didn't pass inspection. "What are you? A lawyer?"

I looked down at my Valentino suit and tie, my polished Italian leather shoes. I shook my head, slightly embarrassed. "No. Do I look like one?" The question was stupid. She and I already knew the answer.

"Yeah," she sighed, still bothered. "You do."

I nodded in agreement. "I used to know…" I started to say,

but my words and thoughts trailed off. They slipped back into my past. Images flashed in my mind like mental postcards. Snapshots of him: Diego Delgado, at the first concert where I first heard him play guitar. In the alley, where we first kissed. On the futon in my old apartment, where we first had sex. In the hotel room in Las Vegas when he told me he couldn't live without me. The far-too-few mornings waking up naked next to the only man I'd ever loved: the guitarist and eventual lead singer of the Jetsetters.

"I like the music," I offered to the woman in the bar.

"Yeah," she said. "That makes sense. It's very retro."

I turned and looked at the blond bartender, who was already chatting with another guy at the opposite end of the bar. "What time is it?" I asked the air around me, not really expecting anyone to answer.

The woman's throaty voice shot back. "Time for you to go."

I nodded and reached for my bag. "You're absolutely right." I stood up and slid an arm through the shoulder strap. The computer bag was heavy.

Just like the regrets you have, Justin.

The cliché made me cringe. The voice inside my head wasn't even creative enough to conjure up a more original or poetic expression to properly capture how angry I'd been with myself ever since I'd made the impulsive decision to slip out of that hotel room in New York and never look back.

I was beyond pathetic and pomegranate martinis, and a one-hour hook up with a Swedish man-whore wouldn't change that.

"Hey," the wild stranger said with a sudden change of tone. "You all right? I didn't mean to piss you off—"

I took a step toward her bar stool perch. "You were *exactly* what I needed."

"Yeah," she said, her glassy expression reflecting my lethal combination of sorrow and self-hatred. "I have that effect on people sometimes."

I glanced back to the bartender, who was too busy flirting to notice me inching toward the exit, toward the terminal.

I wanted to thank the rock-star-in-training sitting at the bar. I thought about hugging her, but I suspected she'd either punch me in the face or laugh her ass off. Instead, I said, "I don't want to be anyone's layover."

She gave a look that said she understood.

I walked away.

The terminal looked like a fluorescent lit maze. I walked against the crowd, following the signs directing me out of the airport, to the world outside, to the City of Angels. I hadn't felt this impulsive in years—if ever. But this was something I knew I had to do.

I was too close to finding out the truth.

I was in L.A. And so was Diego.

This could be your last chance. Don't fuck this up.

The automatic glass doors slid open. I emerged from the airport. I breathed in the balmy evening air, inhaled the overwhelming mixture of car exhaust, smog, and the not-so-distant Pacific Ocean. The rush of it all—the beeping car horns, the amplified reminders of airport parking laws, the passengers stumbling over their luggage—it invigorated me, spurning me on.

I scooted into the backseat of a cab, nearly breathless from the surge of adrenaline pulsating deep in my veins.

"Where ya headed?" the elderly driver asked.

I loosened my tie and replied, "Geneva Recording Studios… on Sunset."

CHAPTER TWO

Had I known I was about to meet the love of my life on that Wednesday afternoon twelve years ago, I probably would've dressed better for the occasion.

I rolled out of bed—or to be more precise, the close-to-the-floor futon—pulled on a pair of torn jeans, slipped on a baggy T-shirt, and laced up a pair of coffee-stained Converse. My hair—an overgrown mixture of toast brown and fading faux punk streaks of burgundy—had needed to be cut for weeks. I skipped shaving, but managed to brush my teeth in less than thirty seconds. I grabbed my keys, wallet, and a never-returned library copy of *Giovanni's Room* I planned to read later on break and bolted out of my closet-sized fifth-floor studio apartment.

Outside, fall was just arriving in Chicago. Golden and rust-colored leaves drifted down into the street like tears shedding for the demise of summer. The air was sharp and stung with a flinching reminder that winter was looming. I shivered a little and silently cursed myself for not grabbing a hoodie or a zip-up sweatshirt to wear.

The coffee shop was only about a three-block walk, which had been a selling point when I rented the shoebox of an apartment. Three years had passed since I'd made my necessary escape from the small town in Georgia by hopping on a Greyhound bus bound for the Windy City. Since arriving, I'd never looked back. I limited phone calls home to holidays and was only reminded of my former life when a random care package would arrive from my holiday-obsessed mother. Or when a customer at the coffee shop caught a hint of my fading rural Georgia dialect when it crept into my words. They would ask me if I was from the South. My reply was usually some variation on *Oh, I spent some time there*.

I landed a job as a barista on the third day of my new life in Chicago. Clouds was a coffee shop independently owned by a lesbian everyone called Starsky. She was petite but fiery, a former radical feminist turned hippie turned small business owner. The only thing she loved more than coffee was her Jack Russell terrier, whom she'd appropriately christened Hutch.

"You're late," Starsky said, without looking up from the morning paper. She was standing behind the counter near a bouquet of fresh wildflowers haphazardly shoved into a blue glass jar. Her curly blond hair was pulled back away from her face and spilled down to the middle of her freckled back in a loose ponytail. As usual, she wore a shapeless sundress and black jazz shoes. I often wondered if she owned anything else.

"I overslept," I explained. I put the paperback on the counter and reached for a white apron hanging from a wooden peg.

"Um, it's one o'clock in the afternoon," Starsky commented after consulting the peace symbol clock on the wall.

I moved around her to get to the espresso machine. "Had a lot of homework last night."

She shot me a look. "What a boring excuse."

I shrugged. "It's the truth."

"Well, I'm Irish and a recovering alcoholic," she reminded me. "At least let me live vicariously through you. You're twenty-two, Justin. Where are your wild stories about being up all night partying with some hot frat boy?"

I shook my head and tightened the strings on the apron, knotting them around my waist. "That's not my life," I said. "That's a porno."

The string of jingle bells hanging from the back of the front door chimed to announce a customer had entered the store. I looked up and felt my breath catch in my throat.

A young Latino guy approached the counter. He was slightly shorter than me and had a smaller frame. His dark hair was messy, wild, and streaked with thick strands of deep violet and vibrant blue. He wore sunglasses, faded jeans, a bomber jacket, and a T-shirt covered with skulls and crossbones. His black combat boots were scuffed and untied. His sweet face was unshaven, but his lips were full and begged to be kissed. His presence was commanding and enigmatic. He demanded attention without saying a word.

But then he spoke. And I was spellbound. "Hey," he said. His warm-as-bathwater voice crept all over my skin, tickling the fine hairs on my arms. The guy had something in his hand, a sky-blue piece of paper with black bold letters on it. It was a flyer for a show—a concert being held that night at a dive bar a few blocks away from Navy Pier. The mysterious young man placed it on the counter as if it were an offering of some sort, something sacred. "I was wondering if you'd hang this up for me?"

I knew Starsky was watching our interaction. I could sense her anticipation as if it were tiptoeing down my back. I felt pressured to prove to her—and to the beautiful stranger—that I wasn't the boring, predictable guy I was perceived to be. I cleared my throat and said, "Are you a musician?"

The guy grinned. His smile was slightly crooked in an Elvis Presley way, but this flaw only made him sexier. "Lead guitarist of Broken Corners. You ever heard of us?"

I felt myself blush. "No," I answered.

The musician raised his sunglasses and revealed his soft hazel eyes. They reminded me of the cinnamon I sprinkled over the tops of vanilla lattes. "I'm Diego Delgado." He offered his hand. I shook it tentatively, careful not to gouge myself with the spiked silver skull ring Diego wore on one of his knuckles.

"Wow," I said without thinking, "your hands are soft for a guitarist."

Diego seemed surprised. He looked down at his hand, studying his palm. "Oh yeah? You shake hands with a lot of guitarists?"

I shook my head. "No…just you."

An expression flickered across Diego's baby face. It was a hot mixture of intrigue and subtle desire. He moved closer to the counter and leaned in a little. "What's your name?" he asked.

I had to swallow before I spoke, as I was certain my voice would crack with nerves. "Justin Holt."

Diego flashed his imperfect smile again. "Justin," he repeated. "I like that."

A few seconds of silence ensued. The quiet moment made me uncomfortably aware of how awkward I felt in my own skin. I reached to the tall tower of paper cups next to the cash register. I almost knocked them over. I steadied them and asked, "Would you like a cup of coffee?"

Diego's smile almost slid into a small laugh. "Yeah." He nodded. "Actually, I would." He reached into his back pocket and pulled out a chain wallet with the word *Hellraiser* stenciled across it in vibrant white.

I filled the cup and presented it to Diego. "Don't worry about it," I said with a gentle shoo of my hand. "It's on the house."

Diego grinned again. "Really?"

I wanted to avoid Diego's eyes because each time I looked into them, a sudden heat crept into my face. Yet I couldn't help myself. Our eyes locked and mirrored lust back at each other. Finally, I spoke again and said, "The least I can do is buy you a cup of coffee."

Diego took the cup and moved to the sugar station—a waist-high counter facing a window offering an obstructed view of an alley and the brick exterior of the florist shop next door. I watched him, studying his movements and memorizing them.

Two sugars. A splash of cream. Marry me, you hot fucker.

Diego stirred his coffee and reached for a plastic lid to cover the cup. "Thanks," he said. He returned to where I stood at the counter. "So...will I see you at the show tonight?"

I felt my hands betray my nerves. They trembled as I reached beneath the counter for a roll of transparent tape and picked up the blue poster with BROKEN CORNERS written across it in block letters. My words felt stuck to the insides of my cheeks. "I don't know...I have...homework...I'm in college...and I read," I stammered.

That's when Starsky stepped in. She suddenly appeared next to me and placed a reassuring hand on the middle of my back. She looked at Diego and said with firmness, "He'll be there."

"Great," Diego replied to her. He returned his attention to me. "Maybe we'll even sing a song for you, Justin Holt." He held my gaze for another second and before he turned away, he added, "To thank you for the coffee."

Diego Delgado walked out of the store. The bells jingled behind him, echoing after his exit. Although the musician was gone, his energy still permeated the coffee shop. It hung in the air like an unspoken double dare.

I moved to the front window with the roll of tape and the poster in my hands. I stared out the window to the sidewalk. I turned my head slightly so I could watch Diego disappear into the jagged edges of the cityscape.

Chapter Three

The air inside the bar was smoky and electric. A crowd of thirty or so strangers mingled around the elevated platform stage. They looked bored out of their minds and buzzed on cheap beer. The audience consisted of skaters and wannabe punkers decked out in what I assumed were secondhand clothes. The black walls were lined with flyers announcing previous shows with band names like Velvet Vultures and Tammy Hates Joe. The grimy concrete floor was stained with cigarette burns and shoe skids.

I stood near the back of the room, sipping on an overpriced amaretto sour. For the last nine hours, I'd been preoccupied with thoughts of Diego Delgado. My fantasies about the hot Latin guitar god were bordering on the verge of obsession. I kept imagining what it would feel like to have Diego's body pressed up against mine, the sensation of feeling him inside me. I craved Diego with an intensity I'd never known.

The lights dimmed in the tiny bar. A stocky butch woman with a jet black crew cut took a seat behind the drums. A rail-thin girl with bone-straight platinum hair stepped onto the stage with a bubblegum pink bass guitar in her hands. She took her position at a microphone off to the left, teetering in a pair of glittery silver high heels.

A moment passed before Diego made his entrance. I felt my breath catch in my throat at the sight of the wild-haired musician.

He was wearing all black. Diego moved to the center of the stage and strapped an electric red guitar over his shoulder.

Then it happened.

A striking woman strutted onto the stage, and the room felt as if it flipped upside down. She was wearing thigh-high leather boots, a pleated skirt barely covering her ass, and a leather studded bolero jacket that did little to conceal a virgin-white bustier. Her hair was a long, thick mass of auburn and platinum-streaked curls. Her lips were painted candy apple red and her cheeks sparkled. Her pale skin glittered beneath the blue lights sweeping across the stage like a desperate searchlight trying to locate a drowning victim.

She faced the crowd, grabbed the microphone, and shouted over their screams of instant adoration, "I hope you're ready, *mothafuckas*!"

The room exploded into a fury of deafening sound. The walls shook from the violent frenzy of the drums and the earsplitting riffs of Diego's guitar. They launched into a fast and furious cover version of Joan Jett's "Bad Reputation." The crowd surged closer to the stage to show their appreciation. They moved in synch with the angry beat, jumping up and down in a wave of throttled movement.

I watched in sheer amazement. Diego played his guitar as if it were an extension of his soul. The female drummer pounded away with a frightening ferocity. The blond pixie-faced bass player looked dazed and high, ready to nod off at any moment despite the adrenaline-inducing music. She never missed a note.

The lead singer oozed charisma all over the stage, knowing very well she held the audience in the palm of her outstretched hand. Her voice was powerful and haunting—sometimes soft and little-girl sweet and then on the next note, ripping into an angry roar.

When Diego joined in on the vocals, his voice wrapped around me and soaked into my bones, flooding my veins with stark desire.

As much as I was infatuated with the hot guitarist on stage, I couldn't resist the allure of the lead singer. From the back of the bar, I hung on her every word as she sang her heart out about unrequited love, the fear of failure, the art of seduction. I couldn't take my eyes off her. And neither could anyone else.

Seconds before the band tore into their final song of the night, Diego looked out into the crowd and scanned the room. He lifted his hand and placed it above his eyes in a half salute, shielding his vision from the unfiltered pink and blue stage lights. The minute Diego saw me—discovered me standing in the back—I felt a jolt beneath my ribs. Our eyes locked and my body trembled on the inside with anticipation.

"We've got one more song for you tonight," Diego said into the microphone. "And some of you might not like us for this, but we don't give a fuck. We're singing this one for you, Justin Holt." With that, the band ripped into a revved-up punk version of the Yardbirds' classic hit "For Your Love."

As Diego's voice filled the room and his declarations of desperate love boomed in my ears, I almost lost my grip on the cocktail in my hand.

Chapter Four

Diego flipped open a Zippo and the flame illuminated the alley behind the bar. He lit the cigarette he held between his lips and breathed in. I stepped into the flickering orange-hot glow. Diego smiled, snapped the metal lighter shut, and exhaled.

"I was hoping I might see you," he said.

I returned his grin and nervously slid my hands into the front pockets of my jeans. "I'm not sure what to say," I offered.

"Say you like our music." Diego leaned against the graffiti-smeared wall and braced himself with one raised leg. The bottom of his black combat boot pressed against the bricks. He stood, posed like a modern-day dark-haired James Dean—the hot Latino version.

Intrigued, I moved closer with the impulse to touch Diego's face, to run my fingertips around the smudged black circles of eyeliner and down to his lips, his neck, to the silver chained dog tags he wore like tin badges of honor. I wanted to slip my fingers through that chain and gently drag him away to a place where the two of us could be alone and spend endless hours pleasing one another.

"I loved the music," I said, but my words were whispered, heartfelt, and not flirtatious.

Diego tapped his cigarette with his thumb and ashes fell

from the tip. They were absorbed into a reflective puddle on the asphalt. He glanced away. I wondered if I was making the oh-so-confident guitar player nervous. "Say that you like *me*," he said. The hope in his voice filled the short distance of space between us.

I reached out a hand. My fingers shook slightly as I placed a palm against Diego's chest, over his heart. "I like you…a lot."

Diego looked down at my hand and then into my eyes. He tossed the cigarette. It ricocheted off the opposite wall and sparked before dying.

"Where is everyone?" I asked. "Your band?"

"They're still inside," Diego answered. "Free drinks. Cheap groupies. Shit like that. A lot of people are into our music all of a sudden and we can't figure out why. We've been getting a lot of buzz lately. I think we're gonna get signed soon. It's about fucking time, if you ask me."

I swallowed. "So…we're alone?"

In response to my question, Diego reached out and grabbed a handful of my T-shirt and pulled me toward him. Our mouths met almost violently as we kissed with a detonated passion. An electric white energy transferred between our bodies, transmitted by the wicked hunger in our tongues. Our movements were primal, savage. We groped, fondled, and pressed. Soon, we found ourselves breathless, panting bursts of rapid air onto each other's mouths.

Diego shifted, turned, and pinned me up against the wall, trapping me with the urgency in his body, the weight of his heavy lust crushing against my frame. He grinded against my hips until our cocks found each other and throbbed through our jeans.

Suddenly, Diego pulled away. He held my face in his hands as if terrified to be separated from my mouth. "I want you," he breathed.

I fell forward toward Diego and the guitarist immediately embraced me. I felt weak, light-headed, overwhelmed.

Emotionally my mind was racing with a thousand possible scenarios: what the two of us could become to each other. Physically, I was surrendering to the unknown, to the almost hypnotic power Diego already had over me.

A throaty, liquor-soaked female voice sliced our moment in half, destroying our deep dive into hot lust. "For fuck's sake, go get a room."

I tried to pull away from Diego, but he tightened his grip around my waist and pulled me toward him. "What's it to you, Brenda?" he said to the lead singer with the bloodshot blue eyes.

"Gimme a smoke," she said, "and I'll tell you how the two of you can be alone together."

Diego reached to the inside pocket of his jacket and fished out the pack and the Zippo. She snatched both from him with a quick flash of a greedy hand. She lit her borrowed cigarette, took a deep drag, tilted her head back, and let a thin line of smoke seep out between her glossy lips. She flicked ashes and they drifted in the alley toward me. She turned and narrowed her eyes, her false lashes blinking slowly like tiny wings. "Who in the hell are *you*, lover boy?"

"He's Justin," Diego said, sounding protective. "He's with me."

"I'm Brenda Stone," she explained. "You the one we sang that corny song for?"

"Guilty as charged," I answered, hoping I didn't sound as giddy as my voice did in my head.

"Is he the coffee-shop kid?" she asked Diego, who nodded in reply. She had gall calling me a *kid*. She couldn't be more than a couple of years older than me. But I knew if I challenged her, she'd probably kick my ass in the alley and embarrass the hell out of me in front of Diego. I kept my mouth shut. I decided to focus my attention on Diego and ignore the Amazonian singer.

That proved to be impossible to do.

"Where you from, loverboy?" Brenda wanted to know.

"He lives here," Diego answered before I could open my mouth.

"How sweet." Her voice was thick with sarcasm and a dirty layer of disgust. "You found a hookup in your hometown, Diego. Too bad this romance will be short-lived."

I turned to Diego and asked, "What's she talking about?"

He let out a soft sigh, defeated. "We're leaving soon," he explained. I felt my heart sink to the asphalt, where Brenda stubbed her cigarette out, grinding it with the back of her boot heel. "We just launched another tour," he continued. "Tonight was our first show."

"For how long?" I asked.

Diego swallowed, looked away. "For five weeks."

"Then you'll be back?"

He nodded, attempted to offer me a small smile. "Yes… well…at least for a while. It depends on what happens. Our new manager says we're on the verge."

Brenda stepped between us, forcing us to separate. She smelled tropical, like coconuts. She handed Diego his cigarettes and silver lighter. "I can cover for you for an hour," she told him. "That's all I can give you, *amigo*. So make the best of it."

"An hour?" he repeated. "We only have an hour together?"

"Take it or leave it," she said.

I slipped my hand in Diego's and announced, "I'll take it."

Chapter Five

Diego didn't say a word to me until we reached the water's edge. Once we were standing on the shore of Lake Michigan, in the shadow of Navy Pier and away from the late-night throng of inebriated tourists, he placed a gentle hand under my chin and lifted my face to meet his eyes. "I don't want to sleep with you," he said. I searched for his expression in the moonlight and offered him a look of confusion in return. "I mean, I do…Of course, I *do*." I could hear the smile in his voice. "Just not tonight. Not like this. Not with me getting back on the road in less than an hour."

The Chicago night air was chilly. It drifted off the surface of the lake, weaving around us like an invisible tease. I shivered a little. "What *do* you want?" I asked. "I mean, what is this, Diego? This connection between us? I know you feel it, too."

Diego shrugged, tucked his fingers into the pockets of his bomber jacket. "I don't know," he answered, "but I think I already miss you and I haven't even left yet."

Then don't go. Stay here. With me. Forever.

I placed my palm against his cheek. His skin was warm and smooth, despite the stubble. "I know you have to go," I said. "It's important. I can tell."

"We've been working toward this for three years. Playing every shitty place they let us. Proving ourselves each time. But

I think it's *finally* going to happen. I think we're about to get signed to a major label."

"Is that a good thing?"

He looked away, toward the never-ending horizon. "It's what Brenda wants."

"But not you?"

I caught a beautiful reflection of the moonlight and the shiny surface of the water floating in his light brown eyes. "I just want to play guitar," he confessed. "That's all. It doesn't matter to me where or how, I just love the music. I always have."

"From what I can tell, you're really good at it," I said.

"Thanks," he replied. "It's the only thing I really know how to do."

"Then do it," I told him. "Go kick ass on the tour."

I hoped we were alone on the beach, that nothing or no one would ruin the incredible moment between us: the sand beneath our shoes, the water rolling back and forth, the moon casting an angelic white glow over us.

He wrapped an arm around my waist and the front of our bodies brushed against each other. "But will you be here when I come back?" he asked.

I almost laughed. "Where else am I gonna go? I hate to break it to you, Diego, but I don't have much of a life. I have school. I have my job at Clouds. I live alone."

I felt the palm of his hand pressing against the small of my back. "Is it unfair of me to ask you to wait for me?"

"Maybe," I replied. "But something tells me that you're definitely worth it."

He kissed my lips and whispered, "All I can promise you, Justin, is that I'll be back in five weeks. And I won't stop thinking about you until then."

I slid my arms around his neck and answered, "Then what more could I ask for?"

❖

We jumped in a cab a few minutes later. Diego directed the near-deaf driver to the Lower West Side of Chicago, to a primarily Latino neighborhood known as Pilsen. I'd never been there before, but I'd heard of it. It had a reputation of being a tough place to grow up. I glanced out the window at the storefront Mexican bakeries and grocery stores as we slid down 18th Street before turning onto a side street and arriving in front of a three-story apartment building.

I waited for Diego to get out of the cab but he didn't. He seemed frozen. I wondered if maybe he was paralyzed by a memory triggered by being in front of this particular place.

"Diego," I asked, "what are we doing here?"

"This is where I'm from," he told me. "This is where I grew up. In there." He pressed his fingertip to the glass and pointed at the building. "I wanted you to see it. To know me. Who I am."

I looked through the window. The faded brick building was surrounded by wrought iron, even the windows. Either the residents were trying to keep outsiders from entering, or living there felt like being trapped inside a prison. "It seems like a nice place," I offered, noticing the front cement steps leading to the main entrance were cracked.

"It's not much, but it's home," he said. "Well, it used to be. My mother still lives there. On the third floor."

"Don't you want to see her? To say hello?" I asked. "Or good-bye?"

"I said good-bye to her three years ago before I moved to L.A.," he said. I heard the faint strain of tears rising in his voice. "I can't go back in there now. It's too much for me to see her. I just look at her…and I can tell…how much she hurts."

"Did you guys have a fight?" I asked, worried I was prying.

Diego took a quick breath before he spoke. "My dad was killed in Vietnam," he said. "It happened during the fall of Saigon."

I met his tear-filled eyes in the dark and said, "That's very sad."

"I never even met him," Diego continued. "He died right before I was born."

"And your mom? Is she okay?"

Diego lowered his eyes. "She bought me my first guitar. On my sixteenth birthday."

"She must be very happy for you. For the band."

"No," he said, shaking his head. "She's never been happy. She gets sick real bad when it gets cold. She hates the winters in Chicago," he said. "She's always wanted to go back to Mexico."

"Why doesn't she leave, then?"

Diego shrugged. "I think she's holding on," he said, "to his ghost. Maybe a part of her is still hoping he'll come home."

My mouth felt dry and my stomach ached. "That's really sad."

Diego shifted in the backseat, shaking off the somber mood. He flashed his crooked Elvis smile at me and asked, "So tell me about you. Where are you from?"

I licked my lips before I spoke. "I'm from a little town in Georgia. Not far from Macon."

"Georgia?" Diego repeated, sounding surprised. "I thought I heard a little bit of a Southern accent."

"It used to be worse, believe me. I've spent the last three years trying to get rid of it."

"What was it like living there?"

"I grew up on a farm," I explained. "We had goats."

"You still talk to them?" he asked.

"To the goats?" I joked.

"No." Diego laughed. "To your parents."

I shrugged. "Only when I have to."

His smile dimmed. "They don't like you?"

"They don't know me," I answered.

"Yeah," he said with a gentle nod, "I feel the same way. I've never really had the family I wanted. But now…I mean, with you…"

I reached for his hand in the darkness of the cab, stirred by the intense look on his face. "With me?"

"With you…everything seems possible," he said. "I was thinking…maybe me and you…we could—"

There was an intrusive ringing in the cab. A cell phone. It rattled the moment, postponed it. Diego slipped the phone out from his pocket, flipped it open, and answered it with a frustrated "Yeah?" He looked at me while the voice on the other end of the conversation spoke to him. His gaze drifted down to our hands and out the window at the place he once called home.

I felt a tremendous sense of sadness swirling inside me. So much had occurred in such a short span of time. Twenty-four hours ago I didn't even know Diego Delgado or that his rock 'n' roll band band even existed. A part of me was elated Diego and I had discovered each other: Fate had intervened and insisted our paths cross. The other part of me was terrified I would never see this incredible man again. If I let him out of my sight, he could be gone for good.

He lives in L.A. now, Justin. Just let him go.

Diego leaned forward and tapped the shoulder of the old guy behind the steering wheel. The cab driver turned down the radio, muting Patsy Cline.

"We're ready to go back," Diego said in the direction of the man's hearing aid.

Diego leaned back and slid his arm around me, pulled me toward him. We sat in silence, drifting through the streets of Chicago.

A few minutes later, we were back at the club, in the alley where a white passenger van was waiting for Diego.

To take him far away from me for five weeks.

Diego leaned into our kiss good-bye. "Promise me you'll be here when I get back."

"I promise," I whispered into his soft lips.

He slid the chain of dog tags from around his neck and

dropped them into my palm, closing my fingers around them with his hand. "Hold on to these for me," he instructed. "Guard them with your life. They belonged to my father."

He kissed me again, slow and tender. I opened my eyes in time to watch him step out onto the broken sidewalk. He closed the cab door and our eyes searched for each other through the glass.

"Pull away slow," I told the driver, who either didn't hear me or didn't care. He floored it and we zoomed away from Diego, leaving him on the curb.

Within seconds, Diego Delgado disappeared from sight. As if on cue, the tape deck in the dashboard clicked to life and Patsy Cline's voice resumed, filling the darkness around me.

Yet I knew there was nothing that could comfort me. There was no song sad enough to mark the occasion.

CHAPTER SIX

I lived in self-inflicted agony for the next five weeks. Each day dragged by like a punishment, intent on constantly reminding me that I'd fallen in love with a man I couldn't have.

At least until he came back to Chicago.

I kept myself as busy as possible, stumbling from one daydream to another. I worked extra shifts at Clouds, allowing Starsky to take a much-needed weekend trip to see her long-distance lover in Madison. I offered to dog-sit for her. I took Hutch for extra-long walks to tire us both out. I spent each night listening to sappy love songs, cleaning my apartment like a bad habit, and doing my homework. Any free time I had, I devoted to finding out as much as I could about the man whose return I was waiting for patiently and faithfully.

The Internet became my new best friend. The more I researched Broken Corners, the more I realized they were on the brink of worldwide fame. Brenda Stone, who had grown up in San Francisco, was a classically trained vocalist. Inspired by her lifelong musical muse Pat Benatar, Brenda turned her back on a possible career in jazz or opera for the glamorous world of rock 'n' roll. Athena Parker, the band's drummer, came across in interviews much more endearing and soft-spoken then her butch stage persona suggested. She was a staunch vegetarian, believed in holistic medicine, and was an advocate for animal rights.

Mary Jane Lewis, the subdued bass player who I suspected was addicted to painkillers, was a former first grade schoolteacher turned band member.

And then there was Diego Delgado. The object of my not-so-secret desires had been born and raised in Chicago. He graduated from a local performing arts high school, where he'd excelled in their music program. He attended college (the same one I was struggling through four days a week) but dropped out after the first semester to pursue a professional music career. There was no mention of his family, a boyfriend, siblings, enemies, or a secret wife. Nothing. The man was a mystery.

Of course, it only made me want him more.

The band had formed in Santa Monica three years ago, and just as Diego had told me, they'd played every dive across the country—more than once. They'd gained a small following, but as far as I could tell they were broke and probably starving, living from one gig to the next.

By the fourth week, I was beyond thinking rationally. Not once did I consider the possibility Diego would return to Chicago for a just few days only to leave again. Somehow, I convinced myself in my lovesick stupor that a relationship between us was not only possible, but destined.

We would be the exception in the music industry. We would be the couple who survived the glare of the public spotlight. We would be the ones who never broke up.

In my mind, there was plenty of room for me in Diego's rock 'n' roll world. I would fill the void in his life perfectly. I would go on tour with him. I would ration out bottles of his favorite ale so he wouldn't get too drunk to play guitar. I would make beaded necklaces for him by hand. Okay, so maybe he wasn't the type of guy who would wear a beaded necklace (not even a choker), so I would light his cigarettes for him, or carry his guitar, or battle off groupies. I would do any and every thing in my power to make him happy. And, in return, he would be inspired to write songs about me. About us. About our happy gay life together.

Eternal bliss awaited us both.

First, he had to hurry up and come back for me.

What I wasn't expecting were the postcards. The first one arrived five days after our temporary good-bye. I found it on the floor of Clouds, slipped through the metal slot in the door and mixed together with the other mail.

The front of the postcard was a scenic photograph of the Atlanta skyline. I turned the card over. It was addressed to me.

> *I'm in Georgia. Atlanta, to be exact. Of course this place makes me think of you. But, then again, everything makes me think of you. Yours, Diego D.*

I studied his handwriting carefully, noticing the way he wrote in all capital letters and dotted his *i*'s with dashes instead of dots. I wanted to lick the postcard, smell it, shove it in my mouth and devour it.

I wanted Diego Delgado. I wanted him *bad.*

From that day on, one postcard arrived for me six days a week like clockwork. Each contained only a few lines of devotion.

> *Van broke down in Tallahassee. Wish you were here with me. Counting down the days. And the nights. Yours, Diego D.*

Each night when I got home, I would secure that day's postcard to the front of my refrigerator, creating a mural of Diego's beautiful words. I would sit on the floor, reading them over and over for hours until my eyes blurred, or I passed out.

Five weeks couldn't go by fast enough.

❖

The stranger sitting at the wooden café table stared at me over the top of her cup of coffee. "Do I know you?" she asked, squinting. She drummed her French manicured nails against the sunflower yellow mug.

I looked over to where she sat in the front window of Clouds. Behind her, the world outside was gloomy and gray. The first snow of the season was in the forecast. It would be another long and lonely chilly night.

I was holding the most recent postcard I'd received from Diego, rereading his brief words for the hundredth time.

I'm in Lubbock. And I think I've fallen madly in love with you. I hope that's okay. Yours, Diego D.

I tucked the postcard into the front pocket of my coffee-stained barista apron and focused my attention on the questioning customer.

She was my age, but sexy and glamorous. She looked like a supermodel: filthy rich, gorgeous tan, an expensive designer purse. Her long, dark hair was curled and held back away from her face with a pair of oversized designer glasses sitting on top of her head. I wondered if she'd snuck inside Clouds to avoid paparazzi chasing her. But no hounding photographers appeared in the window or doorway of the shop.

I'd never seen this woman before. She was captivating. I was instantly intrigued by her.

She crossed her legs and tugged at the hem of her pleated black miniskirt, appearing to be concerned about the amount of flesh she was showing. Her low-cut pink tank top barely covered her breasts. I wondered if she was freezing. Or delusional. Or both.

"I saw you," she continued, as if her memory of me was becoming clearer with each word she spoke. She turned her gaze to an empty corner of the shop, perhaps seeing the moment reenacted in her mind. "In the alley," she recalled. "Kissing the guitar player from Broken Corners. Yeah...yeah, that was *you*."

I moved from around the counter and approached her table, nearly tripping over the untied laces of my Converse. "You know them?"

She smiled at me and her teeth were as perfect as the rest of her.

She should be on a toothpaste commercial. Or selling America bottles of shampoo.

"Apparently not as well as *you* do," she said. "But, yes…I'm a huge fan. Brenda Stone is my personal idol. I live and breathe for that woman."

She gestured for me to sit down with her, so I did.

"I'll be honest with you. I've always suspected that Diego played for the other team."

"I'm not sure what you mean," I said.

"Boys. He likes boys. I mean, you're a boy, aren't you?" I nodded. "Strange…you don't seem gay either."

For some reason, I started to blush. Never before had my sexuality been talked about so candidly. "I don't?"

"No. You look more like a skater. Especially the hair."

I touched my overgrown bangs. "My hair?"

"So, you and Diego, huh? Do tell. Do tell."

I shrugged. "There's not much to tell."

Her pale green eyes narrowed. "He used you once and kicked you to the curb? Wow. He doesn't seem the type."

"No. Not exactly." I slid my fingers beneath the collar of my dark green T-shirt and pulled out the chain revealing the precious dog tags to the wide-eyed stranger as if they were proof that Diego and I liked each other. "We made a promise to each other."

She gave me a strange look and said, "Awwww…that's adorable." I couldn't tell if she was being sarcastic or sincere. Her smile was so convincing it was difficult to detect if evil was lurking behind it. "I hope it works out." She reached across the table and offered me her hand to shake. "I'm Darla Madrid. And before you ask…no, it's not my real name. I invented it."

During the minutes that followed, I learned that not much about Darla Madrid was *real*: her nose, her boobs, her spray-on tan—even her purse was fake.

Yet as superficial and shallow as Darla Madrid was, I welcomed her company. In her, I discovered a fellow lover of all things Broken Corners. While she raved on about how fantastic Brenda Stone was, I was deep in my devoted thoughts about Diego.

"It's settled," Darla declared. "When the band comes back next week, you and Diego can elope, they can finally send Mary Jane to rehab, and I can join the band."

"What instrument do you play?" I asked.

"Other than the stereo?" she wondered aloud. "I think I could handle a tambourine…or one of those triangles."

I struggled to hold back my laughter. Was she kidding? Was this an act?

"Do you sing?" I asked.

In response, Darla stood up, positioned herself in the center of Clouds, like she were taking center stage in a stadium arena. Her mouth opened and her pop-perfect, baby-doll voice filled the shop as she sang a few a cappella lines from the cult classic "There's a Barbarian in the Back of My Car." It was almost as good as the real thing by Voice of the Beehive.

She squealed when she was done and applauded her own impromptu performance.

"Soooooo…whadja think?"

"I think you're…very…entertaining," I answered.

She swooned over my answer, fanned herself with both hands, and gripped the back of the chair she'd sat in just seconds before as if she needed it to prevent herself from falling over from the excitement. "I've always been told that, Justin. Everyone I meet says I'm a born entertainer."

"You have a nice voice."

She sat back down, reached across the table, and squeezed

both of my hands. "I really think it's going to happen for me soon."

I didn't want to burst her enthusiastic bubble, but I had no idea what she was talking about.

"What's going to happen, Darla?"

She lifted her bright coffee mug and raised it in a toast to herself. "Stardom," she breathed.

I reached inside the apron pocket and ran my fingertip over one of the corners of the postcard.

While I knew with certainty that Diego and I were meant for each other, I also had to agree with Darla's prediction: She was born to be a radio star.

It was only a matter of time before we both had what we wanted.

Before our wildest dreams came true.

Chapter Seven

Justin?" the man's voice on the other end of the phone said. "Is that you?"

"Diego," I breathed. At the mere sound of his voice, my body was dusted with chills before erupting into an aftershock of a sweet rush of adrenaline. "It's me."

I was standing behind the counter at Clouds, the old-fashioned black receiver pressed to my ear, clinging to it with such intensity my knuckles turned white.

The shop was empty. Outside tiny snowflakes were drifting down to the sidewalk. Winter was coming, whether we wanted it to or not.

It was noon. I was starving. I spied an almond croissant in the glass display case beneath me. I made a mental note to devour it after finishing with the surprise phone call.

I imagined for a second that Diego was there with me, sitting at one of the wooden café tables and looking up at me with those cinnamon eyes. He was sipping on a vanilla latte and waiting for me to join him.

"My God, I've missed you," he said. His words crawled into my ear. They slid into the emptiness inside my heart, sealing cracks. I sighed. I felt my body relax from five weeks' worth of tension I'd been carrying between my shoulder blades like an invisible backpack filled with hopes. "I didn't know where to find you. I don't have your number. Or your e-mail address. Or nothing. How did I leave Chicago without getting your number?"

I grinned. "I don't have a phone. I can't afford one."

"You need to get one." I could hear the smile in his voice, that crooked grin of his. I couldn't wait to kiss his lips again, taste his beautiful, hot mouth. "Did you get my postcards?"

I nodded as if he could see me. "I sure did."

"I haven't stopped thinking about you," he confessed in a hushed tone. "What have you done to me, Justin Holt?"

I felt myself blush. "Um…the same exact thing you've done to *me*," I said.

"You're too cute," he said. "Adorable."

"Where are you?" I asked.

"I'm *here*." The excitement in his voice was infectious. It made me feel giddy, ridiculously high and euphoric. "I'm in Chicago. We just got here a few minutes ago."

I closed my eyes, allowing the last blast of relief to wash over me. "You're here?"

He made it. He came back for me, just like he promised. Now our life together can finally start. The world can now resume.

"I can't wait to see you," he said, and the urgency in his voice made me ache for him even more. I wanted to be next to him, by his side, in his presence always. Where I belonged.

"Tell me where to meet you," I said. "Starsky should be here any minute. I can leave then."

He took a breath. "We have a show tonight."

"A show?" I repeated.

I'd imagined our reunion would consist of a bottle of cheap but good wine, boxes of Chinese takeout, a few candles, possibly some poetry, maybe a song or two, and an incredible night of passionate sex.

A concert had never entered my thoughts.

"We're opening for a band at the 8-Track. Do you know where it is?"

I tucked away my disappointment and didn't let it seep into my voice. "Yes...yes, I've been there."

"I'll put you on the guest list. After the show, I'm all yours."

"I'll hold you to it, Diego Delgado."

I looked up as the bells jingled on the front door as Darla walked in. She was sporting a new short-waisted faux fur coat and a black and white checkered skirt suit, complete with black vinyl go-go boots. She lowered her dark sunglasses and shot me a glossy smile.

"Uh...Diego? Can I bring a friend with me?" I asked. "She's a big fan."

"Sure. You, plus one. I'll take care of it," he said. "Justin, I have to go. We have to do a sound check. They're calling me."

"Go," I said, trying to hide the reluctance in my voice. "Go do the sound check. I know you're busy."

"You'll be here tonight for sure?"

"I wouldn't miss it for anything," I promised.

"Until tonight, then?" he asked.

"Until tonight," I replied. I hung up the phone.

Darla rushed to the counter. A wave of her sweet perfume crashed over me. "Don't tell me!" she said. "No...screw that...I mean *tell me*! Was it him? It was Diego, wasn't it? He called you? Ohmigawd, are you *dying*?!"

"I hope not," I said, cracking a smile. Darla had that effect on me. I couldn't resist her perpetual state of high-energy optimism. She was contagious.

"The lead guitarist of Broken Corners just *called you*. On the *phone*. Why haven't you passed out by now?"

I shrugged. "Because I like being conscious," I answered. "I don't want you to freak out or anything."

She crossed her heart and then held up her right hand as if she were prepared to be sworn in to testify on her own behalf. She took a deep breath and vowed quietly, "I'll do my best, Justin."

I took a second before I spoke. “Diego put you and me on the guest list for their show tonight at the 8-Track.”

Her eyes widened. She sucked in the air around us. She covered her mouth with a shaking hand and whispered, “I’m calm. I’m calm.”

I laughed at her. “Okay, okay,” I said. “Freak out if you have to.”

Darla let out a round of squeals and threw her arms up in the air in victory. She leaned across the counter, reached for me, and planted kisses on both of my cheeks. Immediately, she started to wipe the lipstick stains off my skin with the back of her thumb, insisting: “Someday when I’m totally rich and famous, I might pretend like I don’t know you, but right now…you…are…the…coolest…friend…*ever*!”

CHAPTER EIGHT

Darla and I waited in the crowd with lip-licking anticipation. The 8-Track was packed to full capacity. It was hot, hard to breathe, and painful. Some guy who was twice my size kept stepping on my foot. I winced in agony and tried my best to keep my distance from him.

"Hey," Darla shouted to me over the rumble of the room. "Do you think all these people are here to see Broken Corners?"

I shook my head. "I doubt it. They're just the opening band."

My theory was proven wrong the second the lights dimmed. The entire crowd moved like a giant wave, swelling and crashing toward the stage. The 8-Track vibrated from the shrieks of highly charged fans. The energy in the room was intense; I felt a ripple of chills skyrocket across my body.

Athena took her seat behind the drums. Mary Jane wandered on stage in glittery platforms, lost and dazed. Somehow she found her way to her microphone and slipped on her bubblegum pink bass guitar. She stared out at the crowd with a blank expression on her face and blinked a few times.

Seconds passed, and there he was. The man I'd made a promise to five weeks ago was standing on stage just above me. He was back, and looking hotter than ever in a short-sleeve black T-shirt and a pair of faded blue jeans. A few strands of his unkempt dark hair hung in his eyes. His bangs were streaked with bright shades of blue and magenta. His hazel eyes were smudged with black eyeliner. He slid his guitar strap over his shoulder and strummed it once. I felt a pang of lust ache inside me.

Now that you're back, Diego Delgado, I will never let you go.

The band ripped into the opening chords of a cover version of Berlin's classic song "The Metro." I knew the song as a bittersweet new-wave ode to love that could never be. Broken Corners took the song and kicked its ass, truly making it their own. Gone were the keyboards. In its place were vicious guitar riffs and throttling drums.

Brenda Stone stepped out on stage with a handheld microphone in her grip. The crowd exploded into a crescendo of idolatry for her. She tore into the song with the rage of a woman with a broken heart. She teased and taunted the crowd with her provocative moves and her empowering desire for revenge on a man who'd done her wrong.

The crowd jumped up and down with a frenetic recklessness, losing themselves to the pummeling rhythm of the song and surrendering to Brenda's quest for justice in the world of rock 'n' roll love.

When the singer reached out to the audience and her fingertips made contact with Darla's desperate, outstretched hand, my friend lost all composure and was reduced to a state of star struck hysteria.

I resisted the impulse to join in with the audience and contribute to the deafening roar of love for the band, but by the second verse of the song, I couldn't help myself.

I locked eyes with Diego, undressing him in my mind and licking the rivers of sweat trailing down the sides of his beautiful face.

I knew it was just a matter of time—just a few hours—before we'd finally be alone together. And I was sure, more than ever, it would be well worth the wait.

❖

"Should I call him?" Darla agonized for what felt like the five hundredth time. Earlier that day, she'd met a stranger in an elevator at the high-end department store where she worked. Like any straight man with a pulse would, he'd asked her out. I secretly suspected their meeting was no accident. Apparently he was some big-time music critic, and Darla was convinced he had the power to launch her into pop stardom. I wouldn't put it past my new friend to have stalked and followed him inside that fateful elevator, so she could flirt her way into a date that she hoped would lead to bigger things for her.

We were standing outside in the dark, shivering together in the cobblestone alley behind the 8-Track. The band's white touring van was parked a few yards away. Aside from Darla and me, there wasn't a soul in sight.

Broken Corners had left the stage nearly thirty minutes ago. We'd slipped out of the club just before the headlining band had started to play.

"Do you like him?" I asked.

Darla thought about it for a second before shaking her head. "No…he's not really my type."

"No?"

"He's short," she explained. "And balding a little bit."

"How old is he?"

She shrugged and looked away. "I don't know…forty, maybe."

"That's almost twice your age, Darla."

"I'm very mature," she insisted. I'm sure neither one of us believed that. Then she had another thought: "Ohmi*gawd*, what if he tries to kiss me? Yuck!"

I grinned. "It might be worth it."

She sighed. "You're absolutely right, Justin. A girl's gotta do what a girl's gotta do."

"Even if that means making out with a short, balding, forty-year-old music critic?"

"His name is Geoffrey Cole and he's more of a reporter than a critic. He has a *column*. All it's gonna take is one mention of my name in it…"

"He'll fall madly in love with you, turn you into a megastar, and you'll have a brilliant career. He'll use you. You'll use him. It'll be a beautiful relationship."

She smiled and nodded, undoubtedly already writing her Grammy Award acceptance speech in her mind. "It could happen," she agreed.

"You should call him, Darla," I told her. "You've been working your ass off at that cosmetics counter for two weeks now without calling in sick *once*. You haven't had one bit of fun. You owe it to yourself."

"My God, you're so smart, Justin. What would I do without you?"

Darla started to walk away. I stopped her with my voice. "Um…Darla, where are you going?"

"To find a pay phone, silly. I left my cell phone in my other purse. I think there's a coffee shop around the corner."

"I realize that I should be able to protect myself because I'm a guy, but you're leaving me *here*…alone in an alley…in Chicago?"

"Don't worry," she said with a wave. "If I come back and you're dead or frozen or both, I'll make sure you photograph well in your coffin."

I flipped her off the minute she turned her back.

The metal stage door flew open as if it had been kicked—and it had, by the heel of one of Brenda Stone's black go-go boots. She stumbled into the alley with an unlit cigarette stuck between her lips and a half-empty bottle of vodka in her grip. She balanced herself by bracing a hand against the graffiti-sprayed brick wall.

Brenda shot me a glance, raising an eyebrow. For some reason, I couldn't stop staring at her false eyelashes and the splashes of silver glitter across her cheeks. She was having a tough time focusing, drunk and unsteady as she was. Her auburn and platinum-streaked hair was a wild mess. She pushed a handful of it out of her eyes and asked, "Rough night?"

"Excuse me?"

"You look kind of pissed off, lover boy. You okay?"

I shrugged and tried to avoid her eyes. Even plastered, she had a piercing steel blue stare. I felt like she could see right through me. Maybe she had the ability to read my mind. "Yeah, I'm fine," I said. "I'm just waiting for Diego. Have you seen him?"

"Trust me. You're all he talks about. I'm sure his *Messssican* ass will be out here soon." Her words were slurred and spittle popped out of her mouth when she spoke. I winced a little, wiped my face.

Brenda gave me another look. It made me feel like I needed to defend myself. For standing in the alley and waiting. For sharing space with her. For breathing. "I'm here with my friend. She should be back any second. She's making a phone call. I don't know if—" I realized I was rambling, so I stopped talking.

Brenda moved closer, peering at me like I was a secret code she was trying to decipher. She squinted. I wondered if I had something on my face and she couldn't figure out what it was. "Tell me the truth," she said. "Are you a reporter?"

I shook my head. "No."

"Musician?"

I almost laughed. "No."

"So, then…you're just a groupie whore?"

I looked her directly in the eye. It was apparent that Brenda was trying to intimidate me. I knew I needed to let her know that wasn't going to happen. Otherwise, she'd walk all over me. If I was going to be a major part of Diego's life, I had no choice but to make Brenda Stone my ally. "No. I'm not a groupie, and I've never been a whore," I replied, adding, "And I'm not really a fan."

She tried to give me a death stare, but her eyes were heavy and wanted to close. "You don't like our music?"

"It's all right," I conceded.

"All right?" she repeated. "No more backstage passes for you, lover boy."

I slid my hands into the front pockets of my hooded sweatshirt and straightened my posture. "That's not really up to you, is it?"

She took a swig of vodka straight from the bottle. "Let me guess," she said. "You're a *matha-ma-tishin*."

"Actually, I'm a barista," I replied. "You know…in a coffee shop, standing behind an espresso machine."

"So you want to be an actor, huh?"

"No," I said. "I'm in my third year of college. I'm thinking about a career in advertising."

"Well, in the meantime, maybe you can help Athena load up our van." Brenda glanced around. Did she lose something?

Her mind, maybe?

"Fuck," she said. "I need to sit down. Help me."

I eased her down onto a stack of empty wooden pallets piled next to a blue metal Dumpster. Vodka splashed out of her bottle and onto her neck. "You're making me spill!" she hollered, shooing me away with a flash of her hand.

Seconds later, a sweetness crept into her eyes. She gestured for me to sit down beside her, grinning like we were the best of friends. I moved cautiously, fairly certain Brenda was capable of striking without notice.

Against my better judgment, I sat down next to her on the pile of pallets, silently praying I didn't get a splinter stuck in my ass.

"I've decided to change our name," she said to me as if it

were top-secret information. "I'm sick of Broken Corners. It's too fucking corny." She took a gulp, then: "What do you think of Sour Kitten?"

I cracked a smile. "Sour Kitten?"

"Yeah…do you think it sounds too L.A.?"

"No. I mean, I don't know really. I've never been to L.A. I'm from Georgia. That's where my family is."

"You're lucky, lover boy."

"Not really. Chicago's is a cool place to be, but I barely make enough to cover my rent and my parents think I've gone completely insane."

"Have you? Is that why you're in an alley waiting for my guitarist? Are you hoping he'll fuck you?"

Don't let her intimidate you.

"Our connection goes beyond that. It's not about fucking."

"Jesus Christ, you're a greeting card. Just my luck. I have a shitty show and I get stuck sitting out here with Pollyfuckinganna."

My anger started to surface. Who did this drunken girl think she was? She was *nobody*.

I stood up and said, "I'm leaving."

She grabbed the sleeve of my black hoodie and pulled me back down. "Wait!" she said. "Don't go."

"If I stay, you have to chill," I ordered. "No more jokes at my expense."

She took a sip from her bottle. "Are you like one of those stalker fans that freak people out?"

I folded my arms across my chest. It was freezing. Diego needed to hurry. "Until five weeks ago, I'd never even heard of you *or* your band," I told her.

"Then you're retarded," she said.

"And you're a miserable bitch," I replied.

My words didn't faze her. She let out a small laugh in reply, and told me, "I'm changing my name to Halo."

"I don't know you very well, Brenda, but you're not the angelic type."

"Halo Kitty Kat and the Sour Kittens," she said. "Whaddya think?"

I tapped the bottle of vodka. "I think you're shitfaced."

"I think you're right." She let out a big, dramatic sigh. She leaned back against the dirty brick wall and announced, "Maybe I should just be Halo Kat."

I nodded in agreement. "That's a cool name."

"Well, then…my name's Halo Kat now. Tell everyone you know."

"Hello, Halo Kat," I said.

She smiled. "Hello, lover boy." She held the bottle out to me as if it were a peace offering. "You wanna drink?"

"No, thanks. I'm fine. My friend Darla had to go call this guy—a critic or something like that. She met him in an elevator and he asked her out. She's a little crazy but—"

"Don't worry about it. Just shut the fuck up and get drunk."

"I don't really drink much," I said.

"Why not?" she asked. "Is there something wrong with you?"

"Probably," I replied.

"Welcome to the town of disappointment…whatever your name is."

"Justin Holt."

Brenda giggled a little. A mouthful of vodka rolled down her chin and between her boobs. She wiped her face with the back of her hand, dropping her unlit smoke and smearing her cherry red lipstick. "I'm sorry for laughing," she said. "Justin Holt sounds like a soap opera name. Like you're the star of *The Young and the Restless* or some shit like that."

"I always thought my name sounded kind of plain," I said.

She closed her eyes. "Plain is good, Justin Holt."

"Is your life glamorous…Halo Kat?" I asked.

"I'm sitting in an alley that smells like cat piss and cigarettes. Yeah, it's really fucking glamorous."

"I think you're a really good singer."

"No…I'm nothing special. There're lots of girls like me out there. I moved to shitty Los Angeles a few years ago. And my life has been ruined since."

"You make it sound like it sucks," I said.

"It does," she said. "The money sucks. The people suck. *I* suck. Be glad you're not in this business. At least we got a new manager. I had to beg that bitch to take the job because she hates me. But we need her…Well…at least I do…" She took another swallow of booze. "Christ, I can't believe I'm telling you this crap. I'm spilling my problems to you. It's a bad habit of mine… talking too much…to anyone who will listen. Even a stranger."

"Hey," I said. "I don't think we're strangers."

"Well, it's not like we're best friends or anything. I just sat down here because you look kind of cool and I am avoiding an interview with Geoffrey Cole. I thought we could share some vodka, chat a little…be my friend for a few minutes and then I'll leave you alone. And when your friend gets back, you can tell her all about it. And then you and Diego can go off and adopt Chinese babies or whatever it is you two fuckers are planning to do."

I smiled. "Darla will probably freak out if she gets to talk to you. She's the one who wants to be a singer."

"God help her."

"Maybe you could give her some advice or something—"

"And tell her what?" she asked. "How shitty this business is? That I'd rather be a waitress at IHOP?"

"Seriously?" I asked.

"I'm over this," she said. "I'm bored with it."

"But it's just beginning for you. Darla said they're even playing one of your songs on the radio now."

"Anyone with tits can get a song on the radio, lover boy."

I looked her in the eye. "Then why do it? Why be in a band

if it makes you so miserable? Clearly you're not doing it for the money."

Before she could answer me, her eyes closed and she either passed out or fell asleep faster than anyone I'd ever met. I shook her a little and tried to wake her up. "Hey," I said. "Halo Kat, are you all right?"

Darla seemed to appear from nowhere. Suddenly she was standing next to me in her faux fur, checkered skirt suit, and vinyl boots, chewing on a mouthful of gum that smelled like watermelon. "I called him!" I jumped at the sound of her voice. "We're getting together tonight. He's interviewing a band and I get to go with him—isn't that cool?" Darla stopped mid-thought and shifted her focus to the drunken singer lying next to me. "Oh my God, what happened to her?"

"I think she passed out. She's a little drunk," I explained.

"A little?" Darla laughed. "She's wasted."

"She drank a lot of vodka."

Darla slipped the bottle out of Halo's limp grasp and inspected it. "She drank the cheap stuff, too," she said. "That's a shame. A girl should know better."

"What should we do?" I asked. "Just wait for someone to come out and take care of her?"

Darla shrugged. "I don't know." She lifted the lid of the Dumpster and dropped the empty bottle inside it.

"Knock on that door and see if you can get somebody out here," I suggested, gesturing to the rusted metal stage door with a quick nod. "Hurry up, Darla. She doesn't look so good."

Darla knocked on the door softly, as if she were terrified her knuckles would bruise. "Hello?" she said to the door. "Soon-to-be-famous people…we need your help out here!"

"Knock louder," I told her. "No one's going to hear you."

The stage door nearly flew off its hinges when an older woman exploded into the alley like a misfired bullet. At first I thought someone's angry mother had somehow gotten backstage and now had found her way to us, and she wanted to ground us for life. She looked like she was running late for a PTA meeting or a craft fair. Her frosted blond hair was cut short in a shag. Her eyelashes were coated with too much mascara. Her dark, stormy gray eyes were narrow and looked mean. She seemed like she was permanently pissed off. She was wearing a bright pink cable-knit sweater over a white oxford shirt, a double strand of pearls, khakis, and black loafers. Was she the lost host of a cooking show? A chaperone for a church youth outing?

Or the band's new manager?

She shoved her way past Darla, looked down at Halo sprawled across the stack of wooden pallets, and spat, "Jesus H. Christ, not *again*!" She lifted her icy stare and locked her tempestuous eyes on Darla and me. "Who in the hell are you two?"

Darla extended a hand. The woman just stared at it, annoyed. "I'm Darla Madrid and I'm a big fan of Broken Corners."

"You mean Sour Kitten," I corrected her.

Both of the women turned to me, blinked.

"Brenda wants us to call her Halo now," I explained. "Halo Kat, to be exact. And she's changing the name of the band…to Sour Kitten."

Darla giggled. The woman fumed.

"Like hell she is. What happened to her?"

I shrugged. "She was just talking to me and she passed out."

The woman placed two fists on her hips. "That figures." She took another look at Halo and shook her head. "I didn't want this job. I still don't want this job."

"But they're a really good band," I said, still not knowing how this woman was related to them. I was too terrified to ask.

"Yes," she scoffed, "but just like the rest of the good ones, they're pissing it all away—before they even have anything."

The metal door creaked open. Diego stepped outside into the moonlight. Immediately his eyes met mine. His face bloomed into a beautiful smile. He moved over to me, and it seemed no one else existed in the world. He slid his arms around me, pulled me close to him, and we kissed softly. I inhaled deeply, breathing in the smell of him. "Five weeks is way too long," he whispered. "Never again."

The woman cleared her throat to get Diego's attention. Out of the corner of my eye, I saw Darla's mouth hanging open, either in awe or envy.

Or both.

"Diego," the woman said. "I hate to interrupt your little meet-and-greet here, but we've got big problems." She gestured to Halo with a quick jerk of her head.

He looked down and struggled to hold back his laughter. "What are we supposed to do with her, Nina?"

"Help me get her back to the hotel and sober her up. We've got an interview with Geoffrey Cole in an hour," she explained. "Here." She handed him some cash. "Put her drunken ass in a cab."

"Can't we just cancel the interview?" he asked.

Nina shook her head. "Not likely. That little prick won't take no for an answer."

"Can you stall him?" I suggested. She shot me a knifing look that told me to keep my mouth shut.

"Nina, there's no way we can get her sobered up. She's been drinking all day," Diego said.

"Just get her out of here until I can figure out what to do," Nina said.

"Me and Justin will take Brenda to the hotel in a cab," he decided, taking charge. "Nina, stay here while Athena loads up the van. It's her turn to be the roadie tonight."

Nina shook her head in disgust and said, "She's not good enough to act like this. I hope you know that, Diego."

"I know," he said.

Her tone softened. "You're a talented guy. You deserve better," Nina continued.

"She's the lead singer of my band," he reminded her. "It's my job to take care of her. And yours."

"Great," she said. "But who the hell's gonna take care of you?"

Diego turned to me. Our eyes locked, speaking silently.

Nina patted the pockets of her khakis like they were on fire. "Jesus H. Christ, where's my phone? Pray God he lets us reschedule this interview." She ripped open the stage door and screamed at the top of her lungs, "Mary Jane, where in the *fuck* is my cell phone?"

Seconds later, Mary Jane stumbled into the alley in pink ballet slippers and denim overalls. Her eyes were heavy and half-closed. Her bone-straight blond hair didn't move, not even in the chilly night breeze that was tumbling down the alley.

Mary Jane handed Nina a cell phone with a slow, fluid movement of her arm. She could have a second career as an underwater dancer. She was a lost mermaid who had come to shore for the single task of pleasing Nina.

"Where's Brenda?" she asked. Her voice was fairy-sweet.

"She's drunk. And we're supposed to call her Halo now apparently," Nina seethed. Her eyes scanned Mary Jane's face, focusing on her sleepy eyes. "What in the hell is wrong with you?"

Mary Jane tried to look away, but it seemed like she was stuck in a vat of invisible molasses. Every movement she made was laborious. "Nothing."

Nina raised an eyebrow. "No?"

"I'm just really tired, Nina."

"Don't lie to me. What did you take?"

Mary Jane leaned back in her ballet slippers and almost crashed against the brick wall of the building. Nina grabbed an arm and steadied her, held her up. I'm not sure if Mary Jane realized she'd almost fallen. I don't think she even knew where she was: what city, what state, what planet. "I just needed something to calm down."

"For fuck's sake, Mary Jane, get in there and sort yourself out."

It took her a few seconds to figure out how to open the stage door. "It's no big deal, Nina," she said to the metal.

"I will deal with you later."

Mary Jane had success with the door and stepped back inside. "Fine," she said before the door shut behind her.

Nina started to pace, caged and wild. She flipped open her phone and pressed some buttons, jabbing at them with her index finger. "Ungrateful bastards," she muttered. She put the phone to her ear, waited, and then said in a pleasant, forced tone, "Yes, this is Nina Grey calling for Geoffrey Cole."

"Justin," Darla said, touching my sleeve. "Geoffrey Cole," she repeated. The expression on my numb face must have told her I had no clue as to who or what she was talking about. "That's the guy I have a date with later tonight," she explained. "He's the guy who asked me out."

"Are you serious?" I said.

"Is this cool or what?" She moved away from me and stepped in Nina's direction. At the sound of Darla's not-so-stealthy approach, the lioness whipped her head in Darla's direction and warned her from coming any closer with her deadly stare. "Excuse me," my fashionable friend said. "I'm Darla Madrid."

Nina snapped her phone closed. "So?"

"So, I think I might be able to help you."

Nina's fists returned to her hips. I wondered if she had a secret identity. Maybe if someone pissed her off enough she'd transform into a female version of the Incredible Hulk. Or shift from Dr. Jekyll into Mrs. Hyde. "Convince me," she instructed.

Darla flipped up the collar of her short-waisted fur jacket and said with pride, "I have a date with Geoffrey later tonight."

Nina raised an eyebrow. "Do you work for him?"

"What?" Darla stammered.

"Are you a reporter?" Nina demanded. "An escort?"

"Um…no…I work in cosmetics. Can't you tell?"

"But she wants to be a singer," I explained.

Nina's eyes turned to me, silencing me. "Doesn't everybody?" she sneered in my direction.

"Take a look at Brenda—"

"Halo Kat," I reminded Darla.

"Halo," she said, correcting herself. "She's in really bad shape."

"That's no secret," Nina answered, glancing over at the passed-out queen sprawled across her wooden throne.

"So," Darla began. "I can spend some time with Geoffrey and keep him…*occupied.* That will give you some time to sober up Halo and—"

Nina didn't have to think about Darla's suggestion for very long. Within the sliver of a second, she grabbed Darla by the arm and insisted, "Come with me."

Nina pulled the stage door open and led my star struck friend inside. Immediately, I thought of Alice's initial descent into Wonderland. Darla let out a squeal of delight, followed by a long, drawn out "Oh…my…*Gawd*!"

"Darla, wait!" I called after her but she was gone.

The metal door slammed shut behind them.

A sudden calm seemed to fall over the alley like a soft blanket.

Diego looked at me and said, "I feel really bad, Justin."

"What for?" I asked.

He reached for my hand and our fingers meshed "All I've wanted to do is spend time with you since I got here," he said. "Do you know how crazy this makes me? You and I have waited for so long to be together."

"Yeah," I agreed. "The five weeks sure felt like forever."

"And now that I'm here…and you're here…*this* has to happen. Drunk Brenda and a stupid interview."

"You have stuff to do," I said. "It's cool. I understand."

I felt his hands on my waist. He pulled me to him. Our mouths met and we almost kissed. Instead, he spoke. "Come with me to the hotel."

"Seriously?" I said. "Won't I just be in the way, Diego?"

He shook his head. "We'll make sure Brenda is okay. I'll cover for her during the interview with that Geoffrey guy, and then you and I can take off."

"Where do you want to go?" I asked. I'm sure I looked like a grinning idiot, but I couldn't stop smiling. Diego had a euphoric effect on me. One touch from him and I was high, drifting like a kite above the alley.

He grinned. "Wherever you want to take me," he said. "I'm all yours now."

My smile didn't fade but a gust of worry brought me back down to the ground.

Yeah, the voice in the back of my mind said, *but for how long will you be mine? I can't compete with this chaos. My life is dull. Boring. Simple.*

I shook the fear away and asked Diego, "Would you settle for some takeout Chinese and a hot make out session?"

He leaned in, kissed my forehead, and said, "I don't deserve you."

"No," I said. "Probably not. But the feeling is mutual."

His grin crept across his face. "Oh yeah?"

I placed a palm against his cheek, looked him in the eyes, and said, "I've never met someone like you, Diego."

He reached up and covered my hand with his. "That sounds like a bad thing."

"No," I said. "I think you're amazing."

"You just like me for my guitar." He stopped. "Speaking of which, let me grab my acoustic. I'll be right back."

He moved to the metal door.

"I'll be here," I said.

"Promise?" he asked, standing in the doorway.

Our eyes locked. It was in that moment my lust, intrigue, and fascination with Diego shifted into something else. I felt it happen.

Standing there in the alley, I fell in love with Diego Delgado.

"I promise."

"I really missed you, Justin."

"Good," I said. "I'm glad. Because I missed you, too."

Diego disappeared inside.

Halo Kat suddenly stirred. She sat up, puked all over herself, and dozed off again.

The stage door opened seconds later. I expected to see Diego standing there with his guitar case in hand. Instead, a very angry Athena was pursuing a very dazed Mary Jane. I had no choice but to witness their confrontation as it happened.

Mary Jane was clutching a cell phone. "I'm just calling my mother," she insisted.

Athena folded her arms across her chest. "Bullshit," she said. Her voice was solid and sexy, resonating with a take-charge attitude. Even in the dim moonlight in the alley, I could see Athena Parker was handsome. With her slicked jet black crewcut, broad shoulders, and a black tank top revealing her solid biceps, I imagined she had a million women chasing after her.

Maybe I should introduce her to Starsky. My boss would fall head over jazz shoes for this woman.

Mary Jane reminded me of a delicate bird. She was a little creature with a broken wing that had slipped out of the nest and was now permanently lost, never to find home again.

She turned away from us and screamed at the brick wall, "Leave me alone!" Her baby-doll voice bounced off the building. Her words and heartache fell at our feet, drifting into the scattered rain puddles.

Athena stepped toward her band mate. That's when I saw the prescription bottle of pills in her hand. She held them out and shook them like a baby's rattle. "What is this, Mary Jane? What is this *crap* I found in your purse?"

"You went through my purse?"

"Lay off the pills!" Athena bellowed. Her voice caused me to wince.

Mary Jane tried to snatch the pills away from Athena, but she was too slow and the drummer's hands were too quick. "Don't tell me what to do, Athena," Mary Jane fumed, clearly not enjoying the impromptu game of keep-away in the alley. "Stay out of my business!"

"This happens to be my business, too! I've worked my ass off to get where I am and I'm not about to let some fucking little pill popper ruin my chances."

Mary Jane broke out into tears. "Don't talk to me like that!"

Athena grabbed both of the blond girl's shoulders. She shook her for a second. I took a step forward, concerned she'd break Mary Jane in two. The bass player flopped back and forth like a rag doll before surrendering to the grip Athena had on her. "Now, you listen to me, Mary Jane Lewis. You get yourself straightened out and you do it now. This band has enough problems with Brenda. We don't need you doped out of your head also."

Mary Jane wiped her eyes. "Athena, I'm under a lot of pressure right now."

"And I'm not? And Diego isn't? There're other people in this band besides you and it means a lot to us, so don't fuck it up."

Athena released her hold. Mary Jane made one more attempt to swipe the bottle from Athena. She lost the battle once again. "I hate you!" she shrieked before going back inside.

Athena started to follow her, shouting, "Mary Jane, I am *not* finished talking to you!" Athena stopped and made eye contact with me. "You're Justin, right?" she asked, her tone and mood shifting.

I nodded, secretly hoping I hadn't pissed her off for something and now she wanted to kick my ass.

She reached out a hand. I shook it. "Athena Parker," she said. "Drummer and former debutante."

"Justin Holt," I replied. "Barista and son of a farmer."

She grinned. "Sorry you had to see that."

"I'm sorry you guys are going through some…stuff," I replied.

She put an arm around my shoulders like we were long-lost friends. "Diego said you two are heading over to the hotel," she said.

I nodded, again.

"Do you think you could do me a favor?" she asked. "I'm kind of caught in a bad situation."

"Sure. What do you need me to do?"

She took a breath and held my curious stare. "Don't tell anyone, but I'm dating Veronica Marie."

I tried to hide my shock, but it was futile. "The supermodel from Brazil?" I said, sounding like Darla's twin.

It was Athena's turn to nod. "Of course nobody knows about us," she explained.

"Of course," I replied.

"She got back from Paris early. She wasn't supposed to meet me in Chicago until tomorrow night," Athena said. "Once you get to the hotel, I need you to go to room 512 and give someone a message for me."

"What sort of message?" I asked, intrigued.

"Can you tell my girlfriend that Veronica Marie is back in town? Tell her she needs to lay low. Move to a different hotel."

"Your *girlfriend*? I thought Veronica Marie was your girl—" I stopped the second the situation became clear to me. "Ohhh," I said, still channeling Darla. "You mean your *other* girlfriend."

Athena smiled again. I wanted to tell her she had beautiful teeth. "Exactly." She laughed. "She's already at the hotel waiting for me. I called but she never answers her phone. I still have to help load up the van. I'm worried that Veronica Marie will get there first, and I definitely don't want *those* two running into each other. Besides, we have an interview with some guy."

"Geoffrey Cole," I told her.

She gave me a look and said, "Excuse me?"

"Your interview is with Geoffrey Cole. He's going out with my friend Darla tonight. That's why she went backstage with that scary woman Nina. They have a plan to stall Geoffrey. That's why I'm out here with Brenda—or Halo, or whatever her name is now. I'm also waiting for Diego. He said he needed to get his guitar and that he was coming right back, and all I want is—" I stopped. I was rambling like an idiot.

"You're adorable," Athena said. "No wonder Diego is so in love with you."

"Really? He said that?" I asked.

She nodded again and asked, "So…do you mind going over to the hotel and giving Rebel Crawford the message for me?"

"No, I don't mind."

"Thank you!" she said, relieved. "You're saving my life."

"You're welcome, I guess."

"Between me and you, I would've asked Diego to do this for me, but he gives me a lot of shit for having two girls."

"Does he?"

"He's ridiculously faithful," she said. "So, I hope you're ready for that sort of thing."

I smiled and nodded.

Athena moved to the stage door. "Just tell Rebel to get another room and put it on my credit card," she said. "I'll find her later."

And with that, she was gone.

The alley seemed to exhale again with relief and exhaustion, worn out by all that occurred there within the last half an hour.

I, too, felt tired and overwhelmed.

What a night, I thought. *And it's not even over yet.*

I longed to be deep beneath a blanket, curled up on my futon in my tiny apartment, tucked safely away. Already I wanted to slip out of this insane world I had stumbled into and return to the simplicity of my boring, everyday life.

But I knew nothing would ever be the same. Now that Diego and I had found each other, there was no turning back.

I glanced up to the sky and searched for a star.

When I couldn't find one, I settled for the moon.

I closed my eyes.

And I made a wish.

CHAPTER NINE

How do we escape?" Diego asked me during the cab ride to the hotel. The three of us were crammed in the backseat. I was sitting between him and Halo with Diego's guitar case pressed against my ribs. The air was hot and stuffy. I felt trapped. I thought about asking the driver if we could roll down a window or at least turn off the heat gusting out of the vents in the dashboard. But the old man was too busy listening to the eleven o'clock news on the radio.

Is it that late already? The night is slipping by.

"All I wanna do is be alone with you," Diego whispered in my ear. He placed his hand in mine. I prayed my palm wasn't sweaty.

Despite the choking heat, the darkness inside the cab made holding hands with Diego seem romantic, even sentimental. But then I turned to my right. I took one glance at the drunken, passed-out mess sitting next to me, and the moment was ruined.

We zipped by Navy Pier, coasted around the edge of Lake Michigan, and soon arrived beneath the bright, twinkling lights of the entrance to a fancy hotel on Michigan Avenue, in the middle of the Magnificent Mile.

Within a matter of seconds, Diego paid the cab driver, had a brief curbside conversation with a blond male bellhop, and managed to maneuver a semiconscious, puke-stained Halo Kat out of the backseat. By the time I crawled out of the cab, the bellhop and Halo were gone. Diego met me on the sidewalk, where he stood gripping his acoustic guitar case.

"Where's Halo?" I asked, momentarily blinded by the Las Vegas–like illumination pouring all over us from the hotel marquee above.

"I paid the guy fifty bucks to take her upstairs and sober her up," Diego explained.

"Poor man," I said.

We were standing on the curb, face-to-face. Strangers moved past us in a constant flowing river of bodies, anxious to catch a train, or get home, or escape the brisk night air.

"So…we're alone for a few minutes," Diego said. "Me and you."

"Until the interview?" I asked.

"Until the interview," he answered. "Then, after…"

"Don't worry," I assured him. "I'm not going anywhere, Diego."

"I hope not, Justin," he said. "It's taken me over twenty-five years to find you."

"I've been warned about going out with older guys." I said.

He grinned. "How much older?"

"You've only got three years on me. I turned twenty-two in September."

"I'm robbing the cradle," Diego said. A chilly wind swept down the sidewalk and slid through the space between our bodies. Strands of his blue and magenta-streaked bangs fell into his face. I fought the urge to reach out and push them away from his warm, dark eyes.

"I'm more than happy to be stolen," I replied.

I don't know if it was on pure impulse, but Diego stepped forward, held my face in his hands, and kissed me softly. As he pulled away, I dared him, "Do it again."

We kissed a second time with more intensity. One of the marquee lights above us crackled, flashed, and died.

"I knew it," he said, glancing up at the blackened bulb with a smile. "We're electric."

"Or maybe just incredibly insane," I offered.

His smile dimmed. "If that's hesitation in your voice, I don't wanna hear it."

"Maybe just a little bit of reality is sinking in," I said.

"I've always preferred magic," he told me.

"I'm not sure..." I began, but words failed me. I took a breath, started again. "I'm not sure...if I fit into your life."

In response, Diego pulled me toward him, wrapped a strong arm around me, and said, "I saved room for you."

"Maybe so," I said, into his neck. "But I never want to be in the way."

"Hey," he said. "Why so serious tonight?"

"I've had five weeks to think too much."

"Me too," he reminded me. "There's a lot of exciting things happening for me—for the band. But none of it matters to me... without you."

"Do you always say such nice things?"

"No," he said. "Sometimes I can be a jerk."

"Is that a warning?"

"I'm not perfect, Justin."

"Neither am I," I said.

He looked deep into my eyes. I caught a glimpse of the sparkling hotel lights reflected in his beautiful gaze. "But we're perfect for each other."

I took a breath and swallowed the rising wave of emotion flooding my throat.

"How long do we have?" I asked.

He looked confused. "What do you mean?"

"I'm assuming you're not staying in Chicago for long."

"A few days maybe. We're waiting to hear about a European tour. And a possible record deal. We released a single independently. Nina says it's getting a lot of airplay and buzz."

I sighed. "Then we should make the most of every second we got."

"What do you wanna do?"

It was then I remembered the promise I'd made to Athena. I needed to pass on the message to her girlfriend. I needed to go to room 512 and have a quick conversation with someone named Rebel Crawford.

"Meet me in the hotel bar in fifteen minutes," I said, assuming they had one.

Diego gave me a strange look, followed by a delicious grin. "Okay," he said. "Why so mysterious?"

"I have to do a fast favor for a friend and then I'll join you," I explained.

He seemed satisfied with that. "Should I order you a drink?"

Yes, please. Or maybe seven.

I nodded. "Absolutely."

"You can tell a lot about a guy from the drink he orders. What's your poison?"

"Amaretto sour," I said.

"Hmm," Diego said. "A little sophisticated. A little sweet. But full of surprise."

"What do you drink?"

"After a few shots of tequila?" he said. "Just about anything."

❖

Loud music was seeping out of room 512, floating beneath the door, and spilling into the hallway. I knocked a third time, harder. Finally, the desperate sound of Juliana Hatfield's voice dimmed and the volume hushed, then muted completely.

The door clicked open. I stood looking down into the cherub face of a petite punk girl in fishnets, combat boots, a pleated plaid skirt, and a tight black T-shirt with the words *45 Grave* stenciled across her buxom chest. Her eyes were heavily outlined in black. Her lipstick was too dark for her pale complexion. Both of her eyebrows were pierced and a tiny diamond stud sparkled on the side of her nose. Her jet-black hair was styled in exact replication of Bettie Page's famous do.

I wondered if Rebel Crawford was a singer. If she wasn't, she should've been—she had the look.

"Didn't you hear me?" she asked. "I said 'come in' like fifty times already."

"I hope this is the right room," I said, even though it so clearly was. "Are you Rebel Crawford?"

Her eyes narrowed. "Yeah, who are you?"

"I'm Justin Holt—"

She made a weird gesture with her hand, circular and fast—a visual cue to hurry up, to get to the point. *"And?"* she prompted me.

"Athena sent me with a message for you."

At the mention of Athena's name, her expression softened, "What did she say? Is she here?"

"She wanted me to tell you Veronica Marie is back early. You need to get another room. She said to put it on her credit card."

She looked like she wanted to punch me in the face. "Are you fucking serious?"

"She said she'd find you later," I reassured her.

Rebel grabbed the sleeve of my black hooded sweatshirt and pulled me into the room. For being so little, she was surprisingly strong. "I don't believe this shit." The door to the hotel room closed behind me with a loud metal click. I swallowed, feeling nervous and more than a little trapped. The room was huge. It wasn't a penthouse suite, but close to it.

How in the hell is Athena affording this place?

"Sorry," was all I could think of to say to Rebel.

"I hate that woman!" she said. She moved around the room like a whirlwind, grabbing clothes, shoes, CDs, magazines. She reached for a zebra-striped train case on the bureau. She placed it in the middle of the enormous bed, near the messy pile she'd created of her belongings, and flipped it open. It was overflowing with makeup, bottles of nail polish, and huge metal cans of hair spray. "No, no—I don't *hate* her," she said. "It's not her fault she's beautiful and perfect and has Athena wrapped around her anorexic finger."

"I don't think she's very pretty," I offered. "She's just… tall."

"Thanks a lot," Rebel tossed at me with a catlike sneer. "I can't help it if I'm short."

"No. I meant—"

"Whatever you do, never agree to an open relationship," Rebel told me.

"Okay," I said with a nod and a stupid grin.

"Seriously, it'll just fuck with your head. You'll end up crazy and pissed off. Just like me."

"Thanks for the advice," I said.

"Wait. Who are you exactly?" she asked, squinting again.

"I'm Justin. I'm…with Diego."

She smiled at me for the first time, since we'd met. *"Ohhhhhh,"* she said. "You're the one he's all obsessed with."

I nodded. "I think so."

"He hasn't stopped talking about you for weeks," she explained. "What the hell did you do to the poor guy?"

"Nothing," I said, with a shrug,

"Damn it! Tonight's our five-month anniversary," she said, still adding items to the growing heap on the bed. "I guess this means I won't be going to Europe with them. Fuck, I need to pack. Will you help me?"

"Uh…sure."

Rebel and I froze then. We heard a woman's angry voice in the hallway, just outside of the room. "This place is a fucking dump! Five-star, my ass!"

Rebel's eyes grew wide. I felt my heart begin to pound. "Oh shit! It's Veronica Marie!" she said. Rebel looked at me, pleading with me to come up with a solution—and fast. "What do I do?"

"Hide," I answered.

"Where?"

"In the bathroom."

We quickly gathered all of Rebel's belongings, scooping them up in our arms, clutching them with our hands: her train case, Sex Pistols purse, tangerine-colored suitcase, and clothes.

I followed her into the bathroom, dropping a high-heeled shoe along the way. Rebel jumped into the shower, clinging to her things. I retrieved the shoe, tossed it into the tub with her, and pulled the palm tree shower curtain closed.

"Don't breathe," I said.

"Get rid of her," she insisted.

I made it out of the palatial marble bathroom just as an electronic key slid into the lock with a click. The door swung open, revealing a group of people. I stood at the foot of the king-sized bed with what I'm certain was a dumbfounded expression on my face.

Veronica Marie's presence was commanding. In person, she was just as glamorous and flawless as she was on the magazine covers she graced. The Brazilian bombshell screamed seduction in a barely-there white miniskirt and white vinyl go-go boots. Her long, dark hair fell in large curls down to the middle of her back and was held back out of her face with a thick silk headband matching the same bright shade as her daffodil yellow frilly blouse. Her skin was sun-kissed brown like she spent her entire life running along the shore of a tropical island.

Because she probably did.

I scanned the other faces as everyone entered the room. Athena. Mary Jane. Nina.

"Oh my God," I heard myself say. "Where is Darla?"

"Who are you?" Veronica Marie demanded, a hand on her

hip. Her stare was so intense and intimidating, I lowered my eyes and stared at the carpet. "Who is he, Athena? And what's he doing in our room?"

"He's Diego's boyfriend."

I looked up.

I am?

"He's just waiting for Diego," Athena continued, becoming more believable with each word. "I told him it was cool if he chilled here for a while. Until we're done with the interview."

"Where is Darla?" I asked again.

Nina let out a sigh of exasperation and rolled her eyes. "She's downstairs with Geoffrey Cole. She's buying us some time."

"Athena, I want to talk to you," Veronica Marie announced. I think she snapped her fingers, but it could've been my imagination. "In *private*."

"I'm kind of tired right now," she said, and forced a yawn to prove her point. "Can it wait until tomorrow?"

Veronica Marie folded her arms across her chest. She was wearing a charm bracelet. I wondered if it was made out of solid gold. "I'm not going to Europe with you," she pouted.

Nina sat down on the bed and crossed her legs. "Look, can the two of you argue later? We need to go over the contracts for the tour. The promoter sent them over for each of you to sign."

"It's always business with you, isn't it, Nina?" Veronica Marie spat.

"That's what I get paid for, Veronica Marie. Now, if you'll excuse me, I have a job to do."

While Veronica Marie and Nina were engaged in a bitch-stare contest, Athena flashed a look of desperation to Mary Jane.

"Veronica, let's go have a cigarette," suggested Mary Jane, who was apparently sober enough at the moment to pick up on Athena's silent cry for help.

"I'm trying to quit," she huffed.

Mary Jane laid it on thick. Her voice was sugar. "Just

come with me. *Please.* I wanna talk to you about something important."

It was working. Veronica Marie's posture relaxed, but only a little. "I'm not in the mood right now."

Athena moved across the room and stood at the wall of floor-to-ceiling windows. "Just go with her," she said. "I'll still be here when you get back."

"Don't tell me what to do, Athena," Veronica Marie said to the back of her girlfriend's head.

I joined Athena at the window. "Wow. Chicago looks so pretty at night," I said, loud enough for everyone in the room to hear.

I dropped my voice to a whisper. "She's in the bathroom."

Athena leaned in. "What?"

Since Athena appeared to be more interested in the view than her, Veronica Marie apparently changed her mind. "Mary Jane, do you want to go downstairs and get a drink with me?"

The blond bass player shrugged. "Sure. There's nothing else better to do."

"Just don't wander too far," Nina said. "The interview is in less than an hour. I don't want you to miss it."

"I wouldn't mind," Mary Jane said. "Veronica, come on, we'll go get you a drink and me a smoke. We can get out of Athena's way for a while so she and Nina can go over contracts. Then we can come back and the two of you can scream at each other all night long."

"Fine," the supermodel steamed. "Whatever."

I waited until the door closed behind them before I rushed to the bathroom door, pushed it open, and said, "It's okay, Rebel. You can come out now."

Rebel tore back the shower curtain to reveal her hiding place.

Athena leaned against the door frame of the bathroom. Her mouth dropped open in shock. "She was in the shower?"

Rebel squeezed by Athena with, "Hi, honey. Come and find me later when you're through playing with your Brazilian Barbie."

"What's *she* doing here?" Nina asked me, if Rebel's existence was my fault.

"Nina, as usual, it's a displeasure to see you," Rebel said. She turned to me. "Thanks for covering my ass. I'll catch ya later."

With that, Rebel slipped out of the hotel room and disappeared, leaving a bathtub full of her belongings behind.

"Athena, you have some explaining to do," Nina said.

"Hey, don't worry about your friend Darla," Athena said to me. "I'm sure she's fine. And thanks a lot for helping me out. I owe you one."

"No problem," I said. "But let me give you some advice. You need to stick to one woman. And my vote is for Rebel."

Athena grinned.

"Any idea where I might find Diego?" Nina asked. "Are you hiding him somewhere, too?"

I locked eyes with Nina and answered, "Not yet."

Chapter Ten

Walking into the hotel restaurant was like stepping back in history. For a brief moment, I imagined I'd somehow time-traveled to Chicago in the 1930s. I almost expected to see gangsters and glamorous gun molls mingling, flirting, and scheming. I could practically feel the sneaky vibe of those brazen enough to risk the wrath of breaking Prohibition laws. The place should have been bursting with an unquenchable lust for life—and sin.

Instead, the restaurant felt ghostly.

The mood and décor in the place reminded me of the bygone era. The room was low lit, illuminated only by the dim glow of the art deco sconces lining the walls. The leather and velvet high-back booths were semicircular, ensuring a fair amount of privacy to its occupants. In the far corner, a platinum blond woman in a scarlet dress stood behind an old-fashioned microphone, doing her best Veronica Lake impression. Bathed in the harsh glare of a single spotlight, she was seducing the few diners in earshot with her throaty rendition of a classic love song by Ella Fitzgerald. Her faithful male piano player was bent over his keys, playing with deep rapture on his unshaven face, as if he were making love to the baby grand.

I stood in the entrance, flanked by potted palms. I glanced down at my oversized sweatshirt and faded jeans, at my Converse shoes contrasted against the glossy black and white checkered floor. I felt underdressed and completely out of place.

But I didn't care.

I scanned the room, looking for him.

To my left, I heard the familiar giggle of Darla Madrid. She was tucked into a booth with a balding man who I assumed was Geoffrey Cole. She was practically sitting in his lap, fawning over him, laughing at his every word. She was teasing the man, tempting him by licking her lips and brushing her fingertips across his arm.

He doesn't stand a chance.

To my right, Mary Jane was nodding off in a booth, sitting across from an irritated Veronica Marie. Mary Jane held an empty glass against her cheek, cooling the fire in her skin. The supermodel was preoccupied with an argument she was having with someone on her cell phone. Her words were muffled, but tense and firm. Veronica Marie tossed back the rest of the cocktail in her hand and slammed her empty glass down on the smooth, shiny tabletop. She raised her arm and indicated she was ready for another with an angry snap of her long fingers.

I continued my search.

There he was.

Diego sat alone in a booth. His beautiful features were hidden by shadows. He looked mysterious, covert. He was my modern-day Humphrey Bogart and we'd somehow found ourselves in the middle of our own version of *Casablanca*.

Two drinks were in front of him, waiting. He took a drag on his cigarette, exhaled. My eyes drifted upward, following the silver stream of smoke. I watched it drift, spiraling up and then soaking into the light on the wall, absorbed by the hungry heat of the pale amber glow.

He looked up as I approached the table.

I stopped in my tracks. I stood there for a moment too long, just staring at him, taking in the sight of him. He was pretty. Soft, even. But it was that bad-boy streak of rebellion lingering in his eyes that drew me to him. It pulled me in.

Closer.

Maybe it was the nonchalant pose he seemed permanently stuck in that I found so attractive. Like nothing really mattered to him, like he couldn't be bothered to care, to sit up straight, to mind his manners. He was just here, coasting through life, breathing charisma and getting by on his irrefutable charm. Living moment by moment, second to second. He was carefree, reckless. He was the epitome of *wild.* There was a lustful flicker of danger pulsing around him like an invisible force field, threatening and warning anyone who came too close.

Even me.

From the second we'd met, Diego was irresistible to me. I couldn't refuse him—and he knew it. We both did.

I was powerless.

"I've been waiting for you," he said, with that adorable crooked grin of his. "What took you so long?"

"I'm here now," I offered.

I slid into the booth and our eyes met.

I lowered my gaze to the amaretto sour sitting in front of me. The sides of the glass dripped with condensation, forming a ring-shaped puddle at the base.

"You're practically a stranger to me," I began.

I felt his eyes on me, so I lifted mine. He gave me a look of frustration before smashing his cigarette out in a glass ashtray. "That's bullshit. We're not strangers, Justin."

"Aren't we?"

He shook his head. "No one knows me better than you do."

"We've spent a total of an hour together since we met," I reminded him.

He leaned forward. Warm light from one of the wall sconces splashed across his face. "Maybe it only took seconds to figure it out," he said.

"Figure out what?" I prompted.

He didn't miss a beat. "That I want you."

I leaned back in the booth and folded my arms across my chest. I was trying to fight him off, to deny the incredible desire I felt for Diego Delgado. I was losing the battle—and fast—and it was obvious. "I don't want to be a groupie," I stated.

"Didn't you read my postcards?" he asked "I meant every word I wrote to you."

"I believe you," I said. "And your words. I liked them."

"I thought you liked *me*, too," he said. "Or am I wrong?"

I took a deep breath before I spoke. "You're actually really wrong."

His jaw tightened. "Then what in the hell are you doing here?"

I looked into his eyes. Even though he seemed angry and tense, his eyes made me feel safe. Secure. Embraced. "I'm falling in love with you," I confessed.

His expression softened. "Justin…"

"You don't have to say anything back…not until you're ready, and not until you mean it. See, it only took seconds for me, too. To figure it out. I don't want to be a one-night stand or a sleazy hookup."

"No," he said. "That's not me. That's not what I'm about. This is *so* much more than that."

"I don't want to be your pen pal in Chicago."

"I've had pen pals before," he said, "and I've never wanted to fuck one of them."

"Is that what you want, Diego?" I challenged. "You wanna fuck me?"

He reached for my hand. He opened it and ran his fingertip across my palm. He was playing me—my body—like I was the strings on his guitar. Touching me with gentle authority, claiming me. The sensation sent chills from the back of my neck down to the soles of my feet.

I shuddered. I tried to pull my hand away.

Diego stopped me, holding my wrist. He was stronger than he looked. Powerful. And I liked it.

A lot.

"I've never wanted someone as badly as I want you," he said. His eyes burned a hole in my skin, singeing every private, dirty thought I'd ever had. I felt like he was devouring me in his mind. Unhinging his jaw and swallowing me alive. "I want to take you somewhere," he continued in a low, hushed voice. "Undress you. Kiss every inch of your beautiful body. Tease you for hours. Pleasure you until you pass out. Then, when you come to again, I wanna hear you ask for it. I want the words to fall out of your mouth. I want you to plead for me to put my cock deep inside you. I want you to beg for me to fuck you. When I think you've earned it, I'll slide inside you—real slow at first—and once your body gets used to mine, I'll pound your ass as hard as I can. I won't stop fucking you until you cry and tell me you can't take it anymore. And I'll make you come…again and again and again. Then, when you've had enough, I'll wrap my arms around you and hold you while you sleep. Because, I know, from that moment on, you'll always belong to me. And I will never want anyone else in this world except for you. Even in our dreams, Justin. You and I will only live for each other."

He reached for his pack of smokes. I watched his hands, his mouth, the illumination from the flame of his shiny Zippo when he flipped it open and sparked the fire. He took a drag, tilted his head back, and exhaled. "So," he said, holding my stare. "What do you say?"

In response, I reached for my drink. By now, most of the ice had melted. A few cubes floated across the top of the tumbler. I wondered if my hands were shaking when I brought the glass to my lips, and if they were—could Diego tell? I swallowed the cool, sweet liquid down in three gulps.

"I don't think I have the power to refuse you," I said. "And you know that."

He grinned. His delicious lips made me want to lean across

the table and kiss his mouth. I resisted the urge. “Good,” he said. “Because I don’t usually take no for an answer.”

“Just don’t use my desire against me,” I said. “Ever.”

I moved. I stood up. I looked down at him.

“I live fifteen minutes from here,” I said.

His mouth curled into an edible smile. He slid out of the booth.

His words tickled my face. “I’ll pay the cab driver extra if he gets us there in five.”

CHAPTER ELEVEN

We couldn't get each other's clothes off fast enough when we stumbled into my studio apartment ten minutes later.

Diego set his acoustic guitar case down on the hardwood floor, slipped out of his bomber jacket, and lifted his black T-shirt over his head. I ran my hands over his smooth torso and stopped for a moment to lick his hard nipples. He let out a soft moan before kicking off his combat boots and tugging at the silver button on his jeans. He stepped out of them and stood in front of me in a pair of plaid boxers and black socks.

Moonlight and patches of flashing neon poured in the tiny windows of the apartment, covering our bodies with a midnight swirl of silver blue and streetlamp gold. I stripped off my hoodie, my T-shirt, and my jeans. I couldn't remember being this turned on before. I slid my underwear down to my ankles and kicked them off. Immediately, Diego reached for my cock and squeezed it.

I led Diego to the futon. I lay down and stared up at him, waiting to feel the weight of his body on mine. Diego stood above me, hovering like a temptation. Slowly, his hands moved to the waistband of his boxers and he gently guided them down, revealing himself to me, while I watched with lip-trembling anticipation. Diego reached down and pulled back the tight foreskin on the head of his cock. He lowered himself, kneeling over me so that his balls brushed against my chest and nipples. He moved his cock toward my mouth and our eyes met as my lips slid over the tip and slowly down the thick shaft. Within seconds, Diego's body started to move. Back and forth he glided, farther and farther down my throat. He reached back and wrapped his hand around my cock and began to stroke me. Our movements soon quickened and heat began to rise off our bodies like invisible steam.

Diego pulled back, slipped his cock out of my mouth, gave it a few pumps with his hand. I reached around Diego for my own cock and jerked it fast.

Diego's eyes closed. My head tilted back. The muscles in our shoulders and chests tightened. Our breaths pulsed until they dissolved into low moans. The first stream of hot come shot from Diego's cock and landed on my lips. My hips bucked just a second before I shot a blast of come across Diego's lower back.

It took a few seconds for us to return from the semiconscious reverie we'd slipped into. When we did, we grinned from intoxicating euphoria. Sweet, nervous laughter tumbled from our mouths. I reached for a discarded shirt on the floor close to the futon and wiped my face with it. Diego rose to his feet and I sat up on my elbows, concerned he'd reach for his clothes and head for the front door. But to my surprise, Diego offered an outreached hand, into which I slipped mine. Diego helped me to my feet. We stood face-to-face and allowed moments to pass. In our silence, it felt as if the world had stopped and nothing else mattered.

Diego leaned toward me until his lips brushed lightly against my cheek.

I moved my index finger up the side of Diego's arm. I traced the outline of a barbed-wire tattoo circling his left bicep.

Diego grinned. "That tickles."

The smile on his face was infectious, glowing from the inside out. The metallic strips of moonlight draped across his body only enhanced this.

Diego spoke and his words surprised us both: "You're beautiful."

For a moment, I felt the urge to cry, not from sadness but because of the tenderness shining on Diego's face. I took Diego by the hand and led him to the bathroom. There I lit two candles and turned on the shower. Within seconds, steam danced around our naked bodies and covered the mirror above the sink with a layer of misty fog. I pulled back the black and white checkered shower curtain and stepped into the clawed bathtub. Diego followed me inside. We met beneath the cascade of hot water. He slid his arms around my waist and pulled me close to whisper, "I wanna hold you."

I draped my arms around Diego's neck and glanced over his shoulder. On the tiled wall, our silhouettes were shadowed by the wavering candlelight.

I smiled at the image of us together, looming larger than life.

It was exactly how Diego made me feel.

❖

We didn't leave the apartment for the next three days. We subsisted on delivered food: Chinese, pizza, sandwiches from Leona's. We ate. We made love. We showered. We talked about a future together. We were fueled by our newly discovered love.

I called in sick, to which a suspicious but pleased Starsky replied, "I hope you mean *lovesick*. As long as you promise to walk Hutch on your lunch breaks from now on, I gotcha covered."

I read passages from *Giovanni's Room* aloud.

Diego played his guitar, including a beautiful version of Bob Dylan's "I Want You."

On the second morning, he was inspired to write a new song he titled "Justin" that started with the line "You bought me a cup of coffee."

We slept side by side, arms and limbs tangled together. We were determined to be as close to each other as possible. We dreamed of the places we would go together; how the world would be a better place to live in now.

We explored each other's bodies with our hands, fingers, tongues, and mouths. We brought each other to the brink of unexplainable pleasure as we quickly discovered our hidden desires. And after each time we made love, I secretly knew in the back of my mind that no one would ever make me feel this way again.

❖

Outside of the apartment, the sun was sliding down beneath the Chicago skyline on the third evening of our seclusion.

Diego sat shirtless in the corner of the one-room apartment, strumming his guitar. A half-smoked cigarette dangled from the edge of his mouth. I was lying stomach down on the futon, skimming through his favorite collection of Pablo Neruda's poems.

The music stopped. Diego took a drag and exhaled a stream of smoke before he looked at me and said, "I know this sounds strange…but I miss my mom."

I raised my eyes from the poetry and said, "You do?"

"Yeah," Diego continued. "I feel bad for her, Justin."

"I'm sure she thinks about you all the time," I said.

"Maybe we could go see her."

I sat up. "Of course we can. Whenever you want."

"I want her to meet you," he decided. "I want her to know you."

"I'd like that, Diego."

"Maybe…it'll help her from being sad so much."

"She still misses your father? After all these years? She never remarried?"

"You know," Diego said, "I never really understood why... until now. Because of you."

"What did I do?" I asked, grinning.

"The song I wrote about you...it came to me because... well, I was thinking...of what I would feel like...if you left me. If I never got to see you again, it would crush me," he said. "Forever."

"Do you think that's how your mom feels?"

He nodded. "I never even met him. He died before I was born."

"I think we should go see her, Diego."

Diego lowered his eyes, back to the strings on his guitar. "I haven't been a very good son to her. I think I left—and never went back—because I hated seeing her like that."

"So fix it," I said. "There's still time."

Diego dropped his cigarette into an almost-empty soda bottle. "You mean before the European tour?"

I felt the color dim in my cheeks. In the midst of our retreat from the world, I'd forgotten all about the impending tour.

Damn it.

"Maybe you shouldn't have blown off the interview the other night," I said. "I'm sure you're in a lot of trouble. Especially with Nina."

Diego shifted his focus back to the guitar. I watched as his hands as he strummed a few chords. "The guy canceled, actually," he told me.

"He did?"

"Yeah. Athena left me a voice mail on my cell phone. I guess something came up at the last minute and he decided to reschedule."

I wondered if that "something" was Darla Madrid.

"I think it was a lame idea anyway," Diego told me. "I mean, why would anyone want to interview us? It's not like we're famous or anything. We don't even have a record deal."

"Yet," I reminded him.

He smiled at me in response. He put his guitar aside and crawled to where I was on the futon. "Why do you look so sad, Justin?"

"Maybe we should talk about it," I said. "The tour."

"What's there to talk about? We leave tomorrow. We'll be gone for twelve days."

"You're leaving. Again."

"Yeah, but this time…you're going with me."

I shook my head. "No can do," I said.

"Bullshit. We'll make it happen."

"How? I have to work all week at Clouds. I have school. I'm interviewing next week for an internship at an advertising agency and I really want the position. Plus," I said, "I don't have a passport."

"Fuck," he sighed. "This sucks."

"But you have to go, Diego. As much as I hate the thought of being away from you again, this is really important."

"If I didn't need the money—"

"I wish I could support us both, but being a barista isn't exactly lucrative."

He kissed my cheek. "Don't worry. Someday, I'll make enough to take care of us."

"What will we do then?"

"Whatever you want."

"Would we go to Los Angeles? Do you have an apartment there?"

"I rent a room from Athena. She owns a condo near the ocean. In Redondo Beach."

"Must be nice."

"Hey," he said, "not all of us can be trust-fund kids. Her dad set her up for life."

"Is her family that wealthy?"

"This band never would've happened without Athena," he

explained. "She takes care of us. All of us. She even paid for all of our equipment."

"Wow," I said. "She must really believe in you guys."

"I think she wants the success more than me," he said. "I just love to play guitar. I'm in it for the music. For the rock 'n' roll. But Brenda is in it for the attention. And Athena…I think she wants to be known as the world's greatest drummer. And Mary Jane…I'm not sure why she's in this. Maybe she didn't wanna teach first graders anymore."

I placed a palm against his face. "I'm in this, too," I promised.

He locked eyes with me. "No matter what?"

"No matter if you have to go to Europe for twelve days. No matter if I have to move to Los Angeles to be with you. No matter if I have to figure out a way to get used to all of this."

Diego slid his hand into mine. Our fingers meshed together. A perfect fit.

"That means a lot to hear you say that, Justin."

"I'm not giving up on you," I said.

"Don't," he replied. "Once we make it big, we can go and live wherever you want."

"Even if I want to stay in Chicago?"

"Hey," he said, "this is my hometown."

"It's the best city in the world," I said.

"You think so?"

"Yeah," I said, "because this is where you found me."

❖

I woke up from a dream that left me feeling panicked. My heart was racing. I felt a thin layer of sweat across my forehead. My lips were dry and cracked. I thought about getting up and grabbing a bottle of water out of the fridge, but the futon was too comfortable to leave.

I didn't know what time it was, but it was dark outside. I searched the room for the familiar red glow of my digital alarm clock. The numbers read 2:55.

The steam radiator in the far corner of my studio apartment hissed and gurgled. The temperature outside must have dropped. December was right around the corner. Winter was looming over us, just like the European tour; the uncertainty of my and Diego's future.

Do we even have one?

God, I hope so.

I took a deep breath and slid closer to Diego's naked body.

His voice sliced through the darkness. "You can't sleep either?"

"Did I wake you?"

"I've been thinking…"

"About what?" I prompted.

He let out a sigh of frustration. "How much I hate the thought of leaving you for twelve days."

I reached for him, his skin. "That's sweet."

"So…maybe I won't go."

I pulled my hand away from him. I sat up, propping myself up on my elbows. "No…Diego…you can't do that."

"Why not?" he asked.

"I won't let you." It was the best answer I could come up with at almost three in the morning.

"It's *my* decision, Justin. They can find another guitarist for the tour."

"But why? No…you can't do this because of me. I won't let you screw everything up."

"I don't wanna leave you."

"I know that."

A wave of emotion cracked his words. "I'm scared."

"What? Why?"

Is he crying? Oh my God, Justin, you made him cry. What an asshole you are.

I lay back down, draped an arm across his stomach.

"I'm scared I'll go away. And I'll come back. And when I do, you won't want me anymore."

"Diego, how can you say that?"

"I'm not an idiot, Justin. You're a really hot guy."

He's insane. Or blind. Or desperate. Or...really, really sweet.

"No, I'm not."

"What if you meet someone else? Someone who comes into the coffee shop. Or at school. Someone who isn't in a band. A guy who can be here with you all the time. Give you what you deserve."

I tightened my hold on him. "I don't want anybody else but you," I said.

I felt his body tense. "It's not fair," he said. "The timing of it all. I want to go on the tour. I want to keep making music. I want to become a better guitar player. But I also want *this*. I wanna spend every second of every day with you. I wanna wake up next to you every morning. I wanna write songs about you. Make love to you. Kiss you all the time. Hear stories about your goat farm in Georgia. I want you to read poetry to me and more books about boys falling in love in Paris. I want us to watch *Like Water for Chocolate*, and go on weekend getaways, and get into arguments at the grocery store."

"You want us to fall in love," I said.

Diego looked me in the eyes. In his, I saw a mixture of sadness and hope. His expression made me ache inside. "I think we already have," he said.

I kissed him gently. "I think you're right."

"Then how, Justin? How do we make this work?"

"You can have it all, Diego. The band. Stardom. Me."

"You're willing to put up with it? With me being away sometimes?" he asked. "Rehearsals and songwriting? Late nights in the studio? Dumbass interviews and publicity? Brenda and Athena and Mary Jane—"

"Yes. And even Nina, too," I said with a smile.

"But is it fair of me to ask you to do this? I mean, you've got a cool life. You like your job and school and your apartment. Then I come along and—"

"Diego, we both know this isn't the ideal situation. You don't have a conventional job. There's no nine-to-five and death by cubicle in your future. That's not who you are. You're a musician—and a damn good one, too. It's your passion. I would never ask you to walk away from it or give it up. I want to be with *you*. And if that means I have to get used to this crazy rock 'n' roll lifestyle, then I will."

He slid his arms around me and pulled me closer to him. I placed my cheek against his bare chest. I could hear the faint thump of his heartbeat. "I don't know what I did right to find you in this world," he said. "I feel like the luckiest man alive."

"Are you kidding?" I said. "You could have your choice of men."

"I've had a few before."

"Then that's a few more than me."

"But none of them were you. I think I knew…that you'd come along soon. I had hope."

"I've been living on hope since I left Georgia," I said. "I stayed busy on purpose. Work. School. They kept me preoccupied. That way I never had time to think about love."

"It's funny when you think about it," he said. "We owe all of this to a cup of coffee."

"Speaking of which, I love the song you wrote about me."

"Maybe it'll be a big hit one day."

I kissed the space above his heart. "Maybe."

❖

We were woken the next morning by an angry knock at the door. I sat up, reached for a T-shirt and shorts, and slid them on.

Diego stirred. "Is someone here?"

"Yes," I said, "and I have no idea who it is."

I started to get up. He pulled me back down to the futon. "Don't answer it. They'll go away."

"It might be important," I said.

He pulled the sheet away from his body, revealing a raging hard-on. "More important than this?" he asked with a sexy grin.

"There's nothing more important in the world than *that*," I agreed. I reached my hand out, wrapped it around his cock, and started to stroke him.

The knock came again, louder and more intense.

"Damn it," he groaned.

I released my hold on him and stood up. "Put something on," I said. "I'm not sharing your beautiful body with anyone."

I waited until he had his black T-shirt and his boxers on before I moved across the claustrophobic apartment and went to the front door.

I caught a quick glimpse of myself in a round mirror on the wall.

My hair was a mess of tangles and cowlicks. My neck was spotted with a fresh batch of hickeys.

What in the hell has Diego done to me?

I pulled open the door and immediately my world shifted. I felt bliss evaporate from life.

Nina stood in the doorway in a trench coat, navy blue skirt suit, and black heels. Her frosted blond hair was damp, as if she'd walked to my apartment in the rain.

"Is he here?" she asked.

I stared at her, confused.

Behind me, Diego said, "Nina, what do you want?"

"It's taken me three days to find you," she said with an angry hand on her hip. "I had to pay a woman named Starsky fifty bucks to tell me where you were." She turned to me with a snarl. "Are *you* the reason why Diego disappeared?"

Diego stepped between us. "Leave him out of this."

"Get your shit," she said to him. "There's a cab waiting downstairs."

"I don't wanna leave," he protested.

She took an aggressive step into the apartment. Her perfume invaded the air in the room. "You don't have a choice. We have a plane to catch."

"Already?"

"Europe isn't going to wait for you, Diego. Now get your shit and let's *go*."

Diego moved away from the door and to his pile of clothes. He dressed quickly and then packed up his guitar. "How important is this tour, Nina?" he asked.

"Very," she spat.

"Playing more dives in the middle of nowhere?"

"I have two contracts for you in my purse."

Diego gave her a look, confused.

"One's for the tour," she said. "The other is a record deal."

Diego was lacing up his combat boots. "Are you fucking serious?"

"You're recording your next single in Amsterdam. If Brenda can stay sober long enough to sing it."

"The deal? Is it a good one?"

She folded her arms across her chest and rocked back and forth in her heels. "It's fair," she said. "Hurry. We don't have much time."

Diego moved as if he were about to leave but suddenly stopped. He reached for my hand and held it. Tight.

"Wait," he said to Nina. "How much time do we have?"

She sighed, irritated. "The flight leaves in five hours."

"Then I'll meet you at the airport."

"Are you out of your mind?" She turned to me, probably as a last resort. "Will you please talk some sense into him?"

"I need to go somewhere first," he said. "With Justin."

"Diego, you'll be back in less than two weeks. It can wait," she said.

"No," he insisted. "It can't. It's important to me."

Nina's cold gray eyes darted back and forth between us. "What's going on here?" she asked.

We stared at her with blank expressions on our faces.

"This isn't some one-night stand between you two, is it?" she said. "You two are serious about each other. I can tell by the ridiculous looks on your faces."

I felt Diego's arm slide around me. "Justin and I are committed to each other," he said. "We're in a relationship."

Nina leaned in close. I could smell maple syrup on her breath. "If anyone finds out about this, it could ruin your career, Diego. Before it even starts," she cautioned.

Diego didn't let go of me. "I'll take my chances."

"You're as bad as my daughter," she said. "Both of you are so stubborn. You think you know what's best."

"Brenda has good instincts," he said.

"Wait," I heard myself say aloud. "Brenda—I mean Halo—she's your *daughter*?"

"Why else do you think I took this shitty job?" Nina answered. "Which reminds me, it's official…we're all supposed to call her Halo now. She wants to file for a legal name change."

"Did she decide to go with Halo Kat?" I asked.

"No," Nina replied. "It's worse than that. Her name is Halo Jet. We've changed the name of the band, too. Broken Corners is dead and gone."

"Sour Kitten?" I asked.

"Thank God, no. I managed to convince my daughter otherwise."

"What's our new name?" Diego asked.

Nina took a breath. I swore I caught a glimpse of money symbols dancing in her eyes. Obviously, the new name was her idea. Part of some big business plan she was brewing. "The Jetsetters," she said, as if it were holy.

I repeated the band's new name in my mind. I had to agree. It was catchy and much better than Broken Corners.

I was in love with the guitarist of the Jetsetters.

With Nina behind the wheel, she'd drive them straight to stardom. A tour in Europe. A new record deal. A hit single.

It was only a matter of time before everyone knew who Diego, Halo, Athena, and Mary Jane were.

"I like it," Diego decided. "By the way, I wrote a new song. I think it's really good."

Nina was ready to leave. Her hand was on the door knob. "Yeah, yeah, yeah," she said. "You can sing it to me on the plane."

She stopped for a second. She looked back at me. "I guess this won't be the last I'll see of you, then?"

I straightened my posture. "No," I answered. "I guess not."

She opened the door. She stepped out into the dimly lit interior hallway. "Then don't fuck this up," she said. "Either one of you. I'll leave a ticket for you at the American Airlines counter at O'Hare."

"I'll make sure Diego is at the airport on time," I promised.

"Good," she said, walking away from us and heading to the rickety, old elevator at the end of the hallway. "I'm glad we understand each other."

I closed the door. I stood motionless for a moment, waiting for Nina's intense energy to dissipate.

Hollowness had invaded my body and I ached from it.

Diego would be gone within hours.

"Hey," he said from behind me. I turned around. Our eyes met from across the room. He was holding the handle of his guitar case. He ran his other hand through his dark hair. His magenta and blue-streaked bangs slipped down again, into his eyes. "I want to take you to Pilsen."

I nodded. "Okay."

He shifted in his combat boots, nervous and anxious.

"I want to take you home with me."

CHAPTER TWELVE

I was breathless and hot by the time we reached the third floor of the apartment building. The narrow wooden staircase didn't look like a tough climb from the ground floor. But once we'd started our ascent, I quickly realized there was next to no air circulating inside the old building.

There was only the overwhelming stench of mildew.

Each step creaked and groaned beneath our feet. I followed Diego, amazed he could take two steps at a time.

By the time we were standing in front of the door marked 3A, I was almost panting. My skin felt like it was on fire beneath my pea coat, scarf, hooded sweatshirt, and jeans. Why had I worn so many clothes, so many layers?

"I don't suppose your mother has an indoor swimming pool," I joked, with a sweaty grin.

Diego gave me a strange look and said, "No such luck," in response.

He reached out a fist and tapped his knuckles against the cracked wood.

I heard a television muted, killing the Spanish dialogue. Then footsteps approached the opposite side of the door. They were slow, padded, tired.

A few locks had to be turned before the door clicked and was finally pulled open—just an inch or two. A pair of dark, heavy eyes peered out at us.

"Dios mío," were the first words I heard Diego's mother say.

"Mom," he said, "Open the door. It's me. I brought someone with me I want you to meet."

At first glance of her son, she dissolved into a puddle of sobs. She flung the door open, threw open both of her arms, and exclaimed, *"M'ijo!"*

Diego beamed in the bright light of his mother's love. He slid into her arms, kissed her cheek, and held her. Emotion crept up inside me and I thought I was going to cry.

Diego's mother was a short, round, and pudgy woman. Her dark auburn hair was graying at the temples and pinned up in a half attempt at a bun. She was wearing a polyester floral printed housedress and faded yellow slippers. Beneath the exhaustion weighing her down, I could see a faint reminder of the beautiful, vibrant woman she had once been. I sensed her sorrow. I could feel it in the air around her. It was a heavy, invisible pillar of heartache she carried across her back, making her every movement difficult.

She couldn't escape it.

Finally, she released her son and looked me in the eye. "Hello," she breathed, taking me in, summing me up, and knowing in an instant everything about me. "You're wit' my son, yes?" Her English was broken, but this made her more endearing to me.

I nodded. "Yes, I am."

"Mom," Diego said, "this is Justin."

She ushered us into the cramped apartment, reaching for us and touching our sleeves. Once we were inside, she bolted three locks on the door. We were standing in the middle of her cluttered living room, surrounded by Catholic artifacts, framed photographs of Diego at different ages, and more knitted afghans than I'd ever seen in my life.

I wondered how many hours of the day she spent stuck inside the cocoon, missing her faraway son and her dead husband.

Diego sank into the low, worn sofa. I sat next to him.

"You look hungry," his mother said. "You don't eat in Los Angeles?"

"Mom, I'm not hungry."

She shook her head. "I'll fix you a plate of food."

"Mom, I wanted you to meet Justin. He's…very important to me, and I—"

She gave me another glance over. Her eyes rested on my Converse shoes. "He looks very hungry, too," she determined.

I stood up. I offered her my hand, but she didn't shake it. "Mrs. Delgado, it's very nice to meet you."

Her hand moved to the beautiful gold crucifix she wore around her neck. She touched it gently. I wondered if she was praying for me. "You may call me Dolores," she said, with a warm smile. "I'm very happy you brought my son home to me."

"He wanted to come and see you—" I started to say, but Diego stood up next to me.

"We can't stay long," he said. At once, her smile dimmed. It was as if someone had unplugged the light inside her soul. "I have to catch a plane in a couple of hours."

"Back to Los Angeles?" she asked, lowering her tear-filled eyes. "So soon?"

If she starts crying, it's over for me. I'll start bawling like a baby myself. How could Diego stay away from her for so long? She's so lonely. And sad.

"No, Ma," he said, "I'm going to Europe."

She turned to me. "You're taking my Diego to Europe?" she said. "Why?"

I shook my head. "No. It's not me. I'm not going."

"Justin lives here…in Chicago."

Her smile returned, but it was faint and not as happy. "Good," she said. "Then he can visit me when you go."

She moved away from us and into a tiny kitchenette, barely big enough to contain a refrigerator, a stove, and a sink. She moved around the sliver of space with expertise.

"She won't let us leave without eating," Diego explained in my ear. "It's just her way."

That's perfectly fine with me, because whatever she's making smells amazing.

"She's so sweet, Diego," I said.

He nodded, watching her. "Yes," he agreed. "She is."

Minutes later, we were handed plates of warm tortillas, Spanish rice, and pinto beans. I inhaled the intoxicating blend of aromas. The combination of smells invoked a sense of comfort and love.

I wondered if I would've brought Diego home to my parents' farm in Georgia, would my mother have snuck off to the kitchen only to return with plates of fried chicken and grits, a pitcher of sweet tea, and slices of sweet potato pie? No, she would've insisted we go out to eat at the local Golden Corral with some explanation like "I'm just not wantin' to clean up a big ol' mess today, darlin'."

Truth be told, the goats ate better than my father and I ever had. Same went for the chicken, cows, horses, and pigs.

"Do you like?" Dolores asked me. She was sitting across the coffee table from us in an overstuffed recliner. The television was on but the sound was still turned down. On the screen, a Mexican woman was crying in what looked to be a scene from a Spanish soap opera.

"It's delicious," I said.

"You come here whenever you're hungry," she told me. She followed my eyes to the television. She smiled "You like the *novelas*? I watch them all night long."

Then Diego did it. He dropped the bomb. "Mom," he said, "Justin is my boyfriend."

She blinked a few times. "What, *m'ijo*?"

Dear God, he's coming out to his dear, sweet mother right in front of me. Where's the door? Can I take the food with me? To go?

"My boyfriend," Diego repeated. *"Mi novio."*

Are you trying to kill her? Is that why we're here?

"Diego," I cautioned. "Maybe you should—"

Dolores leaned back in the recliner and locked her eyes on me. "You are in love with my son, yes?" she asked.

I met her stare. We spoke silently for a few seconds, but I have no idea what we were saying to each other. "Yes," I answered. "Very much."

She stood up and approached me. I looked up, hoping she wouldn't hit me or cuss me out in Spanish. Instead, she took my empty plate and placed a warm, rough palm against my cheek. "Then I will get *you* more food," she said. "And for *me*…the bottle of tequila."

❖

We were sitting on the edge of Diego's childhood bed, facing the only window in the narrow room. Outside, the city was cloudy and gray and on the edge of a snowfall. Inside, the stuffy air was thick with nostalgia.

I traced my finger over a few squares of the quilt beneath us. I knew his mother had made it for him without having to ask.

"It's strange being in here," Diego said to me. "I feel like… I'm sitting in the middle of my past. My mother left my bedroom exactly the same. It's like I never left."

I glanced around the room. Books of poetry—mostly Pablo Neruda—sat in a pile on a makeshift desk in the corner, a poster of Jimi Hendrix was tacked to the wall, a Chicago Bulls jersey hung from one of the wooden bedposts, and a pile of neatly folded clothes filled a laundry basket near our feet. On the nightstand were a clock radio, a Fender guitar pick, and a bizarre lamp with a cartoon cowboy for the base.

"Why did you leave?" I asked. "I can tell you and your mother love each other a lot."

"Because I'm not my father and I never will be," he said. "I look a lot like my dad."

"Yeah, I saw all of the pictures in the living room. I noticed… the similar features."

"As hard as I tried, I could never be him," Diego explained. "That's all she's ever wanted. For my dad to come home. Even though we both know…"

Diego's soft eyes were focused on the view the window offered of the street below us. I wondered how many times he'd sat in this exact spot when he was growing up. How many songs did he write looking out this window? How many plans did he make?

"But it's been so many years," I said. "And she still won't let go?"

"She never will," he said. "He was the love of her life."

With those words, Diego turned to me and placed a sweet kiss on my lips. "You're the only person I've ever brought here," he said. "I was always ashamed of where I come from. It's not very…rock 'n' roll."

I touched his face. "This is your truth."

He shook his head. "No," he said. "*You* are my truth. This here—this is who I used to be. But in you…I see who I want to become."

I felt tears sting the corners of my eyes. "You can't say stuff like that to me and then run away to Europe for twelve days, Diego," I said, fighting back my emotions. The tears won the battle.

"But you know I'll be back, Justin. And while I'm gone, I'll probably write a thousand songs about you."

I nodded. I wiped my eyes with the back of my hand. "I know you have to go." I glanced at the clock, the time. "And you need to go soon, actually."

"Let's make a promise to each other," he said, taking my hand in his. "After this tour, when I come back—I don't ever want us to be apart again."

"Okay," I agreed. "I can live with that."

He slid his arms around me and hugged me. I buried my face

against the warmth of his neck. I inhaled deeply, calmed by the sweet smell of his skin. "Do you know how hard it is for me to leave?"

"Yes," I choked.

He reached for the chain of dog tags around my neck. "I still want you to keep these for me…until I come home to you."

"I won't take them off," I vowed.

Diego stared at me for what seemed like an eternity. His eyes moved across me, every inch of me, slowly. It felt like he was memorizing me.

"I always knew I would meet you," he said. "I just never knew when it was going to happen. But now that I've found you…"

I offered him a smile. "Is this what forever feels like?" I asked.

"Yes," he said. "This is what it feels like to be in love."

❖

An hour later, we were standing face-to-face near a ticket counter at O'Hare Airport.

We hugged good-bye, holding on to each other in the middle of a sea of suitcase-toting strangers. Nothing else mattered to us except each other. The world was an afterthought, just a backdrop for this crucial scene in our lives.

I closed my eyes, not wanting to forget the feel of Diego's body close to mine.

"It's only twelve days," he said, trying to reassure us both. "It'll go by fast. You'll see."

"I'll stay busy," I said. "I'll probably work an extra shift or two. Hang out with Starsky. Get caught up on homework. Prepare for my interview. Anything to keep me from missing you."

He locked eyes with me. "I already miss you, Justin. And I won't stop. Not until—"

I hugged him again, afraid to let go. "You're the most

incredible person I've ever met," I whispered into his ear. "I've fallen madly in love with you, Diego Delgado. You're the most beautiful man in the world. I don't care what we have to go through to be together, I'm yours."

I pulled away from him. The tears in his eyes surprised me. I touched his cheek and wiped them away with my trembling fingers. He reached up for my hand and covered it with his, squeezing gently.

"I've never felt like this about anyone before," he said. "And I know I never will again."

He kissed my cheek.

He stepped back.

We spoke silently with our eyes for a few seconds.

And Diego started to move. I kept my feet planted. The distance between us started to grow. I fought the urge to run after him, beg him to stay, convince him to become a music teacher instead of a rock star.

Instead, I stood in the airport and I cried.

As I watched the love of my life walk away, I already wanted him to come back.

CHAPTER THIRTEEN

Before I met Diego, I never realized how lonely I was, how truly mundane and predictable my life had become. I'd spent the last three years living by rote, repeating the same constant routine until it became second nature. Go to school. Go to work. Come home to my apartment. Eat dinner. Do some homework. Take a shower. Get some sleep.

My life was as simple as the instructions on the back of a shampoo bottle.

When I got home that night after saying good-bye to Diego at the airport, the apartment was resonating with reminders of how alone in the world I was. The only person to whom I mattered was Starsky, and even she'd been preoccupied lately with problems in her long-distance relationship.

As I stood frozen in the doorway of my apartment, peering inside with my key still in hand, I was filled with dread. For the last three days, my world had been constantly filled with a never-ending supply of hot sex and mad love. Diego had gifted me with an incredible amount of affection and attention—and now, it was gone.

I knew I was going to miss him, but *already*, and this much?

What in the hell is wrong with me? I'm lovesick and stupid.

I shut the door behind me and locked it. I took a deep breath, closed my eyes, and silently tried to prepare myself for the twelve days ahead.

❖

Just as I'd feared, everything reminded me of Diego.

I could smell him—on the pillow where he'd rested his head, the bath towel he'd worn around his hips, my skin, my clothes, in the air.

As I lay on the futon, staring up at the cracked, water-stained ceiling of my apartment and aching for Diego, I worried I'd become obsessed with my guitar-playing Latin lover. Somehow, I'd allowed him to take over my every thought.

I reminded myself that even though my life before him was dullsville and suck-worthy, I'd come to Chicago three years ago with a purpose: to create a solid future for myself. I'd saved a lot of money while working at Clouds—mostly bits of change and crumpled bills from the tip jar, but it had added up over time. I only had one year left of college. I was up for an internship at an awesome advertising agency.

I did my best to convince myself I was independent. Diego was lucky to have me. I was a catch. I could get by just fine on my own.

But the truth was, I was completely miserable without him.

I rolled over, buried my face in his pillow, breathed deep, and begged for sleep to come.

❖

"It will be over before you know it," Starsky reassured me a few days later. We were sitting at a café table beneath a ceiling fan. Clouds felt like a deserted ghost town. We hadn't had a customer in almost an hour. Starsky blamed it on the new brand-name coffee shop that opened down the street a week ago. I was more optimistic. I blamed it on the fresh blanket of snow coating the sidewalk.

She was sipping a cup of peppermint tea and nibbling on a slice of lemon poppy-seed cake. I was on my second chai tea latte.

Even though it was the third week of November, Starsky was wearing her usual cotton sun dress and black jazz shoes like summer was just around the corner. At least she had on a pair of white leggings and a knitted scarf around her neck. Petite as she was, I worried she would freeze to death during the three-block walk from the train station to the coffee shop.

It occurred to me my boss was always dressed to teach a dance class. Yet in the three years I'd known her, I couldn't remember ever seeing her dance.

From the wild state of her out-of-control blond hair, I wondered if she'd showered or just rolled out of bed and hopped the "L" train to work. She looked disheveled. Nonchalant. Like she just didn't give a fuck.

"It will be over?" I repeated, and then asked, "Are you talking about life?"

"That, too," she said. "But twelve days is nothing. Sometimes weeks go by before I get to see Sheila."

"Why doesn't she just move to Chicago?"

"Same reason I won't move to Madison. Her life is there. My life is here. It took years before I could open Clouds—a place of my own. I'm not ready to give it up yet."

"Do you think you will?" I asked. "Someday soon?"

"Only if the big guys keep taking away my customers."

"The corporate giants."

"They don't even sell good coffee," she reminded me. "Listen, I know you're missing this guy real bad right now, but give it a day or two. Soon, you'll get back into the swing of things. And before you know it, he'll be here with you. Where he belongs."

"I know," I said, "but then what? He comes back to town for a day or two and then off for another tour?"

Starsky pushed her cake plate away from her. "I don't envy you," she said. "I dated a musician once."

"A guitar player?"

"No. Her name was Annabelle. She was from Switzerland. She played the accordion."

"What happened?"

"Apparently, the accordion wasn't all she played. I got burned. Real bad. I still can't stand the sound of polka music. It makes me crazy." Starsky drifted off for a second, perhaps stepping back into a memory of Annabelle the unfaithful accordion player. I stared at her, wondering how and where she found the strength to survive a succession of broken hearts. She'd suffered through half a dozen breakups since we'd met. "Your guy is different."

I reached for my latte. "How? What do you mean?"

"I saw it in the way he looked at you the first day he came in. He lit up. So did you. It was actually really adorable to watch. The blooming of young love. Which reminds me—we need more wildflowers. The other ones are dead."

"I'll get some tomorrow after school."

"Don't stress too much about your guitar player. If it's meant to work out, it will. If not, enjoy it while it lasts."

"I've never felt this way about anyone before," I admitted. "I feel crazy. Insane."

"You're infatuated."

"Am I?"

"I know the signs. It happens to me all the time. When it wears off, one of two things will take place. You either realize you're in love and it's real. Or you'll want to smash an accordion into a million pieces," she said. "Or in your case, an electric guitar."

"I think I'm in love with him." She gave me a look. "No…I *know* I'm in love with him."

"Then fight for it," she said. "And don't give up."

"Even if that means moving with him to Los Angeles?"

"You'll do what's best for you. I know that about you, Justin."

"Thank you," I said. "I'm glad one of us has faith in me."

Starsky pulled the half-eaten slice of lemon poppy-seed cake back toward her and resumed picking at it with a fork. "Thursday is Thanksgiving," she said.

"Oh, shit."

"Now, is that any way for a pilgrim to talk?" she asked with a grin. "I'm making a tofurkey."

"You're making what?" I asked.

"It's a healthier alternative to a turkey. It's made with soy. Tofu. Shit like that."

"Since when did you become such a health nut?"

"Since Sheila said she hated lesbians who were vegetarians."

"Are you purposely trying to make her mad?" I asked.

"No," she explained, "I'm proving a point. She's not as in love with me as she claims to be. The tofurkey threw her over the edge."

"She's not coming for the holiday?"

"She said she'd rather have a traditional holiday. I told her to shove tradition up her pseudo-Republican ass."

"So then why go through with the tofurkey?"

"At this point, it's a matter of pride."

"I hate the holidays," I groaned.

"Hutch and I insist that you join us. Otherwise, you might suffer from loneliness. And I don't want to be alone either. So it looks like it'll be just you and me, kid."

"I'll bring wine," I offered.

"None for me," she said. "But feel free to knock yourself out with a big bottle of vodka. Remember…my drinking days are long behind me. Five years of sobriety this January."

I had a flashback of Halo Jet sprawled across the stack of pallets in the alley behind the 8-Track, drunk and cradling her bottle of vodka.

And the mess she was in the backseat of the cab.

"I've decided to boycott vodka for a while," I explained. "But amaretto might do the trick for me…and ginger ale for you."

CHAPTER FOURTEEN

I heard Darla Madrid in the department store before I saw her. I was at the Clinique counter, contemplating buying a bottle of Chemistry for Diego for Christmas. My mind was almost made up to forgo the cologne and continue my search for something a little more rock 'n' roll, when I heard the ring of my glamorous friend's contagious laughter. It was a haughty sound really, sweet and high. Sugary. It was almost convincing, but she hadn't yet mastered the knack of making it seem authentic. It spoke volumes to its recipient. Within seconds, if the person she was laughing at was clever enough, they'd realize Darla wasn't really amused at all. Instead, her laugh was just another way of saying "Good God, I'm so much better than this idiot who's talking to me right now."

I followed the faux giggle until I found its source.

Darla stood in a narrow aisle, surrounded by designer purses. She had her glittery cell phone pressed to her ear. She was wearing a pair of oversized sunglasses, a pink cashmere beret, a white scarf, and matching mittens. Her winter coat was unbuttoned, revealing a low-cut white sweater, black pleated miniskirt, and thigh-high go-go boots. She was either Christmas shopping or late for a new job as a pole dancer.

"Darla?" I said.

She turned her head slowly, raised her sunglasses above her

pale green eyes, looked me up and down, tossed a handful of her raven hair over her shoulder, and said, "What are *you* doing here?"

"Um…shopping," I said. "It's a department store. Are you working?"

She snapped her flip phone closed without saying good-bye to whoever was on thc other line. She gave me an evil look. "Are you kidding? I quit this awful job three days ago."

"You did?" I asked. "Why?"

"Haven't you heard? I got a record deal. They gave me an advance and everything."

"That's awesome. Congrats."

"Geoffrey Cole is my personal manager now."

I noticed a new blinding ring sparkling on her left hand. "Is that all he is?" I joked with a grin.

She rolled her eyes and folded her arms across her chest. Apparently, she'd lost her sense of humor. "I agreed to marry the son of a bitch if he jump-starts my career. The man works fast, let me tell you. He was on the phone within ten minutes. And within an hour, I was in a lawyer's office signing my name on the line."

"So when do you start recording?"

"Next week," she said. "They're flying me to New York, which is why I'm here. I thought I could find something decent to wear, but apparently, I was wrong."

Something had clearly happened to my friend. Gone was the fun-loving, thrill-seeking, star-struck Darla. She'd been replaced by an arrogant cutthroat bitch. I wanted to tap her on the shoulder and ask, "Where's my friend? What have you done with Darla? May I please have her back now?"

"How's Diego?" she asked, with more than a hint of irritation lingering in her tone. Was talking to me a chore? "How's the band?"

"They're in Europe."

"You didn't go?" she asked.

I shook my head.

Would I be standing here catching death stares from you if I had?

"Let me guess. You'd rather stay here in freezing-cold Chicago and spend your holidays in misery feeling sorry for yourself in that ridiculous coffee shop?"

I looked at her in disbelief. Had she sold herself to Satan to get her record contract?

"You should've gone, Justin," she said. "No idea what Diego is up to in Europe. One of those French boys might start to look *really* good to him once he gets lonely."

It took every ounce of willpower I had to not reach out, grab both ends of her winter white scarf, and tug as hard as I could.

Instead, I knew exactly what needed to be said, how to make my point. To remind Darla Madrid of who she was, who she'd always be.

"Well," I said, "whenever Geoffrey Cole moves on to the next ambitious girl with no talent, let me know. I'd love to be there for you to help pick up the pieces. After all, isn't that what friends are for?"

As I walked away, Darla exploded into a temper tantrum, attacking every purse within reach with her bare hands. "You just wait, Justin! You'll see!" she shrieked, swinging and hitting. "I'm going to be *famous*!"

❖

As I headed to the "L" train station to return to the sadness of my studio apartment, Darla's words started to sink in like heavy dread.

Within seconds, I felt my body start to break out into a hot sweaty panic. I wiped my brow with the back of my hand and continued down State Street.

Maybe Darla was right. Diego was gone. I was stuck here. His life was moving forward at breakneck speed. Mine was stagnant and dull. How could my world ever be appealing to Diego? Who was I kidding?

What did I have to offer an up-and-coming rock star? He was a Latino sex god. I was a skinny white guy who was often mistaken for a Mormon missionary whenever I wore a white oxford and a tie. I wasn't glamorous or cool or edgy or bitchy. I was a barista. A college student. I was a reject seeking refuge from my redneck heritage, trying to shed my Georgia accent with every word I spoke. I was an imposter. A runaway.

I was nothing.

Out of sight, out of mind.

A horrible scenario began to swirl in the dark pools of my imagination. Maybe Diego would be tempted to fall in lust with some French-speaking fan named Jacques or Pierre, or even Jacques Pierre. Diego would be drawn in by the accent. They would walk the streets of Paris—just like I was walking the streets of Chicago. But *I* was alone, trudging through ankle-high snow. They would be together, strolling through the City of Light, feeling the warmth of the Parisian sun against their skin. Holding hands. Exchanging glances. Sharing bites of Brie and a baguette in a park where a street artist would paint their portrait, while a beret-wearing mime would perform his usual routine in the background. They would make love every night in Jacques Pierre's industrial loft overlooking the entire city of twinkling lights. In the spring, they would propose to each other at the top of the Eiffel Tower. They would have a simple ceremony, somewhere in the French countryside. They would wear matching rings, matching tuxedoes. *They're a match made in heaven* is what their wedding guests would say while they watched the two lovers share their first dance to an Edith Piaf song. Months later, they would open up a French bakery and business would boom. Diego would teach guitar lessons to French children on the side, not for money but because he loved music *and* children. They would take summer trips to the Riviera, or even Monte Carlo. In the years to come, they would adopt French babies and raise them to embrace a bohemian lifestyle—much like their fathers had when they fell in love during the Jetsetters' first European tour.

Seconds before I reached the stairs to the "L" station, I heard it coming from the near distance. The sound was distinctive and haunting. I turned and saw her. She was young and dark-haired, tattered and dirty. She was standing on the opposite street corner, her instrument in her hands. She was playing with the hope that the strangers passing by would drop bits of change into her grimy white mop bucket. Maybe by noon she'd have enough to buy a cup of coffee or a bowl of soup.

Or a bottle of Jack Daniel's to kill the chill and sorrow inflicting her tortured soul.

I know her pain.

But it was the sound of her instrument that struck me, causing me to freeze in my tracks. The music made me realize that if I didn't do something—something crucial—the risk of really losing Diego was growing greater with every day we were apart.

The accordion had never sounded so awful to me before. So out of tune. So annoying, like a desperate screech from the universe.

I listened to the message in the music, immediately reminded of Starsky's story of her cheating, accordion-playing lover Annabelle.

Infidelity? He would never cheat. We made a promise to each other.

Maybe I'd set my standards too high. Maybe we were too young to even consider a serious, committed relationship. Maybe it was my fault for falling in love with a musician.

The reason I'd fallen in love with Diego didn't matter. I

knew just from the strained, earsplitting notes of the stranger's accordion that I had no choice.

In order to be with him, and to love him completely—to give our relationship a fighting chance—I had to leave my life far behind.

CHAPTER FIFTEEN

The night before Thanksgiving, I found myself standing in front of the door to Dolores Delgado's apartment, holding a store-bought pumpkin pie in my hand. My stomach was filled with fluttery nerves. I took a deep breath, knocked gently, and waited for her to answer.

What am I doing here? Why?

My decision to make a seemingly spontaneous visit to Diego's mother wasn't an impulsive one. Well, not entirely.

Once my concern for her began brewing, it only took a few minutes to convince myself that going to see her—even if for a little while—was the right thing to do. Tomorrow was a holiday. She was a widow. She could be my future mother-in-law. I had no choice—I *had* to go see her.

I was in Dominic's looking for the perfect bottle of something to take with me to Starsky's for our planned holiday tofurkey dinner the following day.

I had my hand wrapped around the neck of a bottle of amaretto, poised above my otherwise empty shopping cart, when I saw her. She was an older woman with a haunting expression of loneliness in her sad eyes. Like Dolores Delgado, she was heavyset and looked Hispanic. Her dark hair was pinned up in a loose bun. It was streaked with lines of white, as if someone had taken a dipped paintbrush to her hair. She was wearing a pale pink turtleneck, a lemon-colored cardigan a few sizes too big for her, and lavender polyester pants. She looked like she had jumped out of an Easter basket. She was coming toward me, pushing her cart slowly, moving as if she were permanently wounded and brokenhearted. She looked up. Our eyes met briefly.

The sound of my own voice surprised me. "Hello," I said, as if we were old friends.

Her mouth curled into a warm smile. Her eyes glowed with instant joy. "Hello," she breathed, delighted by my attempt to make contact with her, to establish a connection between us, if only a short one. Her voice was like an embrace. It was gentle and comforting. It made me miss my grandmother, who died when I was eleven. I'd rarely thought of her since.

"Happy Thanksgiving," I said, raising the bottle in some sort of strange salute to her.

At the mention of the holiday, the light in her eyes dimmed a little and her smile faded. "I hope it will be a nice one for you," she said, before moving on.

Within seconds, the sad stranger was gone, off to another aisle, back to her life. But her sorrow hung in the air, choking and smothering the hope and happiness right out of me.

Immediately I thought of Dolores. I wondered if she'd be spending the holiday alone, filling the hours with an endless marathon of *novelas* and flipping through photo albums, staring at the fading face of her beautiful ghost. Had a kind neighbor invited her over for the holiday with promises of a hot plate of turkey, mashed potatoes, and gravy? Was she going to leave the solace of her apartment, trudge through the snow, and make her way to a local Catholic church? Would Diego find a way to call his mother from Europe? Would he remember? Would he care?

I hadn't heard from him since he left. Not one word. No postcards. No e-mails. No phone calls.

Maybe it was out of fear that I paid for my items, left the store, and slipped into the backseat of a taxi. I rode to Pilsen with a pumpkin pie in my lap, a bottle of booze at my side, and an avalanche of anxiety burying my heart alive.

I wouldn't have admitted it had anyone asked, but I was scared Darla Madrid was right. Even though she'd transformed into the biggest bitch in the Midwest, her words had triggered a sense of terror in my already anxious mind. Without reassurance from Diego, I was convincing myself the imagined affair he was having with the fabricated Jacques Pierre was fast becoming a reality. I was positive I was now a distant memory, just another notch in his leather spike-studded belt. I couldn't compete with Paris. Gorgeous groupies. Hot French guys. Adoring fans with adorable accents.

I was just boring Justin Holt: the Chicago college kid who didn't know any better and made the oh-so-ridiculous mistake of falling in love with a soon-to-be rock star.

I should stick to making coffee and homework. It's safer that way.

Earlier that day I'd aced the interview at the advertising agency. I was almost certain the six-month internship would be mine. I knew I'd impressed the panel of three men and two women who threw questions at me like grenades. I caught each one in my teeth, chewed it up, and spat out the perfect answer. They sat across from me in the boardroom in their suits and ties, skirts and heels, eating up my desire to become the most successful copywriter in advertising. They nodded their heads, showered me with smiles, and when I wanted them to laugh, they did. I convinced them my lifelong dream could never happen without them. They had the expertise and the industry knowledge I desperately needed to take my life and career to the next level. All they had to do was hire me, become my personal mentors, and shoot me straight up the corporate ladder.

I knew I wouldn't hear from the college internship coordinator until Monday, so I had all weekend to wait for the company's decision. But if my prediction turned out to be true, my entire life would change direction. I would have to leave Clouds in order to meet the demands of the hectic schedule at the agency. I would be poised for a career. A real job. A grown-up life.

I would have to make a lot of sacrifices.

One of which could be love.

❖

Dolores Delgado pulled her apartment door open just an inch. She peered at me through the crack. It took her a moment to recognize me. Once she did, she unlatched the gold chain from the door and pulled it wide open. She was in a pale pink nightgown and silky robe. I wondered if her old slippers had stayed on her feet since the last time I was there.

She glanced around me eagerly. "Diego?" she said, with a hope that made my heart ache. "Is he here? Did you bring him to me?"

I shook my head. "No, señora. Diego isn't here. He's still in Europe. It's just me."

Defeat filled her face and her shoulders sank. She placed a palm against the front of the door, possibly drawing some sort of strength from the cracked paint and the tarnished *3A*.

I held out the pie. "Tomorrow is Thanksgiving," I said.

She nodded. "Oh, yes. It is."

"I wanted you to have this," I said. I felt awkward. Out of place. Foolish.

She has no idea what you're doing here, you dumbass.

"For me?" she asked, surprised. She took the pie. Her fingers grazed across my knuckles. "But why?"

I had no reasonable answer to her understandable question, so I just stood there in her doorway with a stupid smile stuck on my face.

"Did you make this for me?" she asked.

"Yes," I lied. "I did. Just for you."

We stood there for what felt like an eternity, exchanging uncomfortable expressions and glances. Finally, she broke our silence with a question. "*M'ijo*, would you like to come inside?"

Leave her alone. Turn around. Go back downstairs. Catch a cab. Take your ass home to your apartment and wait to hear from Diego. He'll be back next week, you idiot.

"I would love to," I heard myself say.

She reached for the sleeve of my charcoal gray pea coat and pulled me into her apartment. She closed the door behind us. She balanced the pie in one hand and mastered two dead bolts and the gold chain with the other.

"Oh shit," I said, realizing I'd left the bottle of amaretto in the cab. The driver would be ensured a happy holiday now, at my expense. It was the ultimate tip the night before a holiday.

She gave me an odd look. "What is it?" she asked.

"I forgot something in the cab."

"Do you need to go?"

I ignored the hope in her voice and pushed on. I peeled off my wool gloves, unknotted my plaid scarf. "No, it wasn't important."

We were standing in the middle of her cluttered living room. I breathed in deep, inhaling a combination of dust, oregano, cumin, and damp radiator heat. "Wow. What smells so good?"

She pointed to the couch. "Sit," she insisted. "I will fix you a plate."

I obeyed her command and sank into the worn sofa. I turned my attention to the television screen, where a gorgeous Latina woman in a wedding dress was crying her eyes out. I was intrigued at once by her state of heightened emotions, her beauty, her suffering. No wonder Señora Delgado was addicted to these shows. I was hooked in a matter of seconds.

All around me were framed photos of Diego at different stages of his life. I grinned at the sight of him, feeling at ease and comforted. I stared at the pictures, taking in the history of his life before he met me. While he was here taking care of his mother and coping with her crippling depression, I was in Georgia, feeding goats and dealing with two parents who treated me like a guest who'd worn out his welcome long ago.

"I'm leaving," I'd told them three years ago. I was standing in our living room, with suitcases in hand and a bus ticket to Chicago tucked under my arm.

My mother didn't take her eyes away from the television. My father glanced up from the sports section. "Well, all right, then," he said. "You know what's best, son."

A commercial break came right before I closed the door. "Would it be all right if I convert your bedroom into a craft room?" my mother said to the back of my head. "I've always wanted one of those."

I didn't answer her. I kept walking. I never looked back.

Dolores Delgado didn't look right when she returned with a plate of food for me. Her cheeks were pale and a thick layer of sweat coated her forehead. I scooted over and she sat down next to me on the sofa. She folded up the sky blue and white afghan and tossed it into the seat of the recliner.

"Is everything okay?" I asked. My fork was aimed and ready to dive into the delicious plate of chicken, beans, and rice.

She nodded and reached for the gold crucifix on the thin chain around her neck. *"Sí, m'ijo. Está bien."*

I started to eat but I could feel her eyes on me. I knew she was wondering why I'd come to see her. Strangely enough, I was asking myself the same question. What was I doing here in her overstuffed apartment? How dare I interrupt her deep depression, her night of *novelas* and nostalgia?

I should've had the decency to let her suffer in peace.

Yet she was only part of the reason I was there.

Sitting in the living room made me feel close to Diego. I was surprised by the wave of sadness swelling up inside me.

"I'm very sad today. I miss my husband very much," Dolores

confided in me. She turned and looked me in the eye and asked, *"Tú también?"*

I put down my fork and placed the plate of food on the marred coffee table. "I'm sorry, Señora Delgado," I began. "I shouldn't have come here and bothered you. It's just…I miss Diego a lot. He's been gone for over a week now. I thought maybe if I came here…"

She reached out and placed her hand over mine. Her skin was soft but cold. "Sometimes when I am very sad and I miss my son," she said, "I go and sit in his room."

I nodded. I stood up. "May I?" I asked.

She answered with a nod. She leaned back into the sofa and shifted her gaze to the television screen, drifting back into a fictional world that was safe.

I moved across the apartment until I reached the closed door leading to Diego's past. I turned the brass knob and it clicked. The door creaked with a high-pitched groan as I pushed it open and stepped inside.

The sight of his bedroom made me smile: the Pablo Neruda books on the desk; the Jimi Hendrix poster on the wall; the Chicago Bulls jersey hanging from one of the wooden bed posts; the laundry basket filled with clean, folded clothes; the cartoon cowboy lamp on the nightstand.

I sat down on the edge of the bed in the same spot I'd shared with Diego just days before, facing the window. The breathless view of the Chicago skyline glimmered back at me. The sight of it filled me with a rush of awe and love. I felt invincible. I felt like the best was yet to come. I felt like my fears and worries about a future for Diego and I were put to rest.

I knew he loved me.

And I knew I loved him.

I lay down on the bed and pressed my face deep into the pillow. It smelled old and musty. There wasn't a trace of Diego's scent left.

He turned his back on this place a long time ago. Just like you did when you walked out and left Georgia behind you forever.

I closed my eyes.

I wanted to tell Diego how much I understood him. I knew what it was like to grow up in a place where nothing you saw or touched ever reflected who you were. To find yourself existing in a house of strangers whom you forced yourself to love because that's what you're supposed to feel for your parents. But Diego and I had something in common: Our families had failed us. His mother was consumed with grief. Mine couldn't wait to redecorate my bedroom.

Just like me, Diego was looking for a sense of home, a place where he truly belonged in this world.

I couldn't wait to share my discovery with him, to tell him about our connection and the parallels in our childhoods. Secretly I hoped he'd be so inspired by what I'd realized that he'd write a song about it. I would insist he sing lead vocals on it. Halo would never be able to comprehend where it came from, the organic reasoning behind it. Only Diego's voice could do our song justice.

❖

I must have drifted off to sleep.

I sat up, alarmed and confused. I had no idea where I was.

What time is it?

I heard the television in the distance. Spanish words and phrases floated from the living room and crept beneath the bedroom door.

Wait. The door's closed. I didn't close it.

I felt embarrassed for a second, realizing Dolores must have found me fast asleep in her son's bed and closed the door so the TV wouldn't wake me.

My face was hot. My skin was sticky and damp with sweat.

A rush of dread and panic raced through my veins. I felt an overwhelming sense of doom. Something was wrong. I could tell it. I could feel it.

Get up.

I stood. I moved to the door. I pulled it open. Bluish white shadows from the television screen flickered on the living room wall like silhouettes of monsters roaming through the apartment on the hunt for something to devour.

Dolores was asleep on the sofa, curled up beneath the afghan. I moved closer, contemplating whether I should wake her or just leave.

A clock on the wall revealed it was just after two in the morning. I'd been asleep for over five hours.

I thought about going back to Diego's bedroom, crawling into bed, and falling back asleep, but the peaceful expression on Señora Delgado's face made me freeze with fear.

She looked calm. *Too* calm.

I reached for her. I touched her arm. Ice cold.

"Dolores," I said. My voice cracked with the truth of the situation. I already knew. "Señora Delgado."

I shook her harder. No response.

No. Please, God. No.

"Dolores, wake up!" I demanded, gripping her arm.

I let go.

I turned away from her, banging my knee against the sharp edge of the coffee table. I winced in pain. I reached for the cordless telephone on top of the television. I pushed buttons. I tried to dial. There was no tone. It was dead.

Just like her.

"I don't know what to do," I said to the wall of Diego's photographs. His eyes were pleading with me to do something. To try and save his mother.

I rushed to the front door. I yanked the gold chain so hard it broke into tiny pieces and scattered across the wooden floor. I struggled with the stubborn dead bolts, willing and begging them to work with me. Finally, I yanked the apartment door open and the chilly air in the hallway hit me in the face.

I raced to the first door I saw. I pounded on it with my fists, begging for someone to answer. To help.

To reassure me everything was going to be okay.

But in the back of my mind, I already knew.

Nothing would ever be the same.

CHAPTER SIXTEEN

Diego's voice cracked when he spoke. I could see tears spilling down his cheeks from where I sat in the front row of the church. He stood behind the pulpit, bracing himself by clutching the sides of it. He looked weak. Damaged. "My mother died of a broken heart," he told the dozen people who were scattered in the seats in the ornate Catholic church in the heart of Pilsen. "She never got over the death of my father."

Diego glanced at the blown-up photo of his parents, perched on a wooden easel not far from where he stood. It was a snapshot of them from their younger years. Dolores was sitting in her husband's lap, with her arms draped over his shoulders. She was looking directly into the camera and smiling, but Diego's handsome father was staring at his beautiful wife. The deep love in his eyes made me ache inside. No wonder she never stopped missing him.

They're together now. In heaven.

Those were the exact words I'd said to Diego when he arrived an hour ago. We met on the snow-covered steps of the church. Both of us were wearing ties, blazers, slacks, and shiny leather shoes. We looked like we'd escaped from an all-boys school.

We began to cry the second we touched. He climbed out of the back of the cab and locked eyes with me immediately. He rushed up the cement steps of the church, slid his arms around me, and pulled me to him. We collapsed into a rumble of tears of sadness and relief.

"I'm so sorry," I said into the heat of his neck.

"I got here as fast as I could," he explained. "The plane just landed an hour ago."

"You're here now," I said. "That's the important thing."

"My mom…" he choked.

I held him tighter, afraid to ever let go. "She's with your dad now, Diego. They're together now. In heaven."

He nodded. He wiped his eyes. He kissed my cheek. "So are we," he breathed.

I reached up and removed the chain of dog tags from around my neck. I'd worn them religiously since Diego had entrusted them to me as an unspoken vow of our love. I placed them into his open palm and closed his fingers around them. "You should wear these today," I said.

Diego nodded in agreement.

Behind him, Mary Jane and Athena emerged from the same cab Diego had arrived in. Athena paid the driver and helped an emotional Mary Jane up the stairs to where Diego and I stood. She leaned in and whispered in my ear, "He's gonna need you now more than ever."

I nodded in reply.

I didn't ask where Halo was. Or Nina.

I slipped my hand into Diego's. He led the four of us into the church. We bowed our heads in unison as we entered the sacred place.

Now, as he stood in front of everyone with his heart breaking open wide, I wanted to be with him. I needed to hold him, to assure him that somehow everything would be okay. Even if we knew those words might not be true.

I fought the urge to walk up the carpeted steps and stand beside him in the shadow of the overbearing crucifix looming from behind the sanctuary.

I looked up at the pale yellow walls and the arched stained-glass windows. In one of them, Jesus was nailed to a giant cross. I wondered how God could let something like this happen.

Behind me, I could hear Athena shift uncomfortably in her seat. Mary Jane sniffled and blew her nose.

Starsky was sitting next to me clutching my hand. Maybe she knew I was on the verge of falling apart. I drew as much strength as I could from her energy pulsing against my palm.

If she hadn't taken control of the situation from the second I called her and told her that Diego's mother was dead, none of us would have made it through the tragedy. Maybe she realized she was the only one really capable of handling it all.

Once I finally convinced someone to open their door and to call for help, it took another twenty minutes for an ambulance to arrive. Once the paramedics confirmed Dolores was dead, I went back to the neighbor's apartment and telephoned Starsky. I could barely get the words out, but once I did, she was by my side within fifteen minutes.

Within hours, she tracked down Nina in Europe and explained what had happened. She promised Starsky that Diego would be on the next plane home. Yet he didn't show up for three more days.

I wondered what had happened to him in those three days, but I figured he would explain later.

Starsky made all of the funeral arrangements, including selecting a cherrywood casket. She insisted on coming to the church early to tie bouquets of wildflowers to the end of each pew.

That's just the kind of woman she was.

❖

As we walked away from Dolores's fresh grave in the cemetery, Diego stopped me. We turned toward each other beneath the bare branches of a weathered oak tree. He took my hands into his and said, "I don't think I'll ever be able to forgive Nina for what she did."

I probably looked confused because I was. What did Nina Grey have to do with the death of Diego's mother? "What do you mean?" I asked.

"She waited for two days to tell me," he explained. His jaw tightened and a flash of anger darkened his otherwise light hazel eyes. "She waited until the tour was over. She knew if I found out, I would've left."

I was floored. "She didn't tell you?"

He shook his head. He tightened his grip on my hands. "Not until yesterday, Justin. I can't believe…you had to go through all of this without me."

"It's okay."

"You were there with her when she…died? In the apartment?"

"Yes," I answered. "It was the night before Thanksgiving. I went to see her. To give her a pie," I said. "Pumpkin. And she was alone. So I sat with her for a while. She made me a plate of food. We watched a *novela* for a few minutes. The one about the woman who's forced to marry a man she doesn't love just to save her family's ranch."

"And then what?" he prompted.

"I told her I missed you. She said whenever she missed you, she went into your bedroom. So…that's what I did. I sat on the bed for a few minutes. Then…I fell asleep thinking about you. About us. I woke up. It was late. I thought she was asleep. But she wasn't."

Diego turned away from me and faced the icy trunk of the tree. "I should've been there," he said. "You know I didn't want to go on the tour. I hated leaving you. I won't do it again, Justin. I can't take being away from you."

"Every second of it was agony for me," I said. "Twelve days have never felt so long."

He faced me again. I reached up and pushed his electric blue, magenta, and black bangs away from his tear-filled eyes. "Who did all this?" he asked. "The service? The funeral? The flowers?"

"Starsky took care of everything."

"But why?" he said. "She doesn't really even know me. Or my mom."

"Because she's my friend, Diego," I said. "Not everyone in this world is like Nina."

"I don't know how I can look her in the eye now," he said. "I'm so angry with Nina. How can I work with her?"

"Can't you just fire her?" I asked. "She hates her job anyway."

"Are you kidding?" he said. "Now that we've got the record deal and they shipped out our new single to every radio station in the country, there's no way we'll get rid of her. She's milking us for every penny she can make. She gets twenty percent of everything. We all signed the contracts."

"I understand she has a business relationship with you and Athena and Mary Jane, but to make a profit off her own daughter… that's disgusting."

"It's all about money now," he said. "It's not really about the music anymore. We haven't even started to make some noise in the industry and I'm already sick of it. I just want to write some amazing songs and play some kick-ass guitar…just like Jimi did."

"And Halo? What does she think about all of this?" I asked. "Why isn't she here, Diego?"

"Brenda's in rehab," he said. "She needed to sober up for a few days. She drank so much in Paris, she puked all over the stage during our show. The club owner wanted to sue us but Athena paid him off. It was a bad scene. The three of us threatened to quit the band unless Brenda cleaned up her act. Nina forced her to go to some place near the beach."

"So, then…what now? What's next for you guys?"

He sighed. “Another tour.”

I felt my body tense up immediately. “How long?” I asked.

“Twenty-four cities in five weeks. Las Vegas is up first. Then Los Angeles. New York. After that…who knows?”

“Five weeks?” I said. “I’m not going to see you for five weeks, Diego?”

I feared his answer. School was over until January. I would be completely alone. The only thing I’d have to keep me occupied was work.

I’ll work extra shifts. I’ll find a hobby. I’ll buy a fucking cell phone.

I felt his palm against the small of my back. “No,” he said. Our mouths were only inches apart. “You’ll see me every day.”

“I don’t believe you,” I said, staring him in the eyes.

His lips curled into that delicious crooked smile I found so irresistible. It was impossible to refuse him when he turned on his charm. “I’ve already made the arrangements,” he said. “You’re coming with me.”

❖

Diego and I retreated to my apartment after leaving the cemetery. We didn’t say much. We didn’t kiss. We loosened our ties, peeled off our sport coats, kicked off our dress shoes. We curled up next to each other on the futon and fell fast asleep.

I dreamed he and I were in the apartment he’d grown up in. It was night. I was sitting on the worn-out sofa. Diego and his mother were dancing together around the living room, bumping into the wooden edges of furniture, knocking over pictures, laughing. I cheered them on, clapping and stomping my feet. The song they were moving to was in Spanish. I couldn’t understand a word of it, but the upbeat energy of the music made me happy.

Mother and son hung on to each other, breathless and smiling, speaking silently with their eyes. I never wanted them to let go.

The sun was just starting to rise over the city of Chicago

when Diego and I were woken up by the electric buzz of his cell phone. He rolled over and reached for the phone on the floor.

"Hello?" he said. His voice was heavy and gruff. "Yeah... we'll be there."

I stood up and moved to the coffeemaker in the kitchenette. "Everything okay?" I asked once his brief call had ended.

"How fast can you be packed and ready to go?" he asked. "That was Athena. We have to be to the airport by nine."

I glanced at the clock on the wall. "I can make it," I said. "I need to call Starsky, though. I don't want to leave her stranded. She's depending on me to be there to help out at Clouds."

Diego moved to me. He pressed me up against the edge of the counter. I could feel heat generating from his body. "*I* need you with me," he said into my mouth. His kiss felt angry, almost violent. He pulled away from me and moved toward the bathroom.

A few seconds later, I heard the squeak of the shower faucet and the usual thud in the water pipes as they sprang to life.

I turned toward the cabinet and reached for the canister of Folgers.

Chapter Seventeen

I wasn't expecting Darla Madrid to be in Las Vegas, but there she was in a white faux mink coat, a sparkly pink tube top, rhinestone-studded cowgirl boots, and a mirrored miniskirt that reminded me of a disco ball. Her dark hair was huge and barely moved, sprayed into place within an inch of its life. She was wearing big sunglasses and way too much perfume. She looked like she'd crawled out of an '80s heavy-metal music video.

Whitesnake, anyone?

Darla picked at her fake bubblegum pink fingernails and sighed every few seconds to remind all of us how incredibly bored she was. When that didn't get her the attention she was craving, she crossed—and uncrossed—her legs repeatedly. Each time she offered a free peek at the asset she'd used to land herself a record deal and a manager/fiancé who was twice her age and half her height.

She hadn't said one word to me in the five minutes we'd been in the same room. She refused to make eye contact with me, even though I gave her death stares from where I sat, a few feet behind the members of the band—sans Halo. Nina stood near the exit door, hovering over her musically inclined meal tickets like a pterodactyl. Diego sat between an irritated Athena and an overmedicated Mary Jane.

Geoffrey Cole was short and squat. His little feet barely

touched the goldenrod-and-burgundy carpet of the empty ballroom in the hotel. He was shoved into a cheap suit and tie, sitting in a metal folding chair with a yellow legal pad balanced on his knee and a stubby pencil clenched in his meaty hand.

We were the only ones in the oversized room. On other occasions, I'm sure the ballroom was a great location for conventions, seminars, and wedding receptions. Today, it was the meeting place for an interview between a new band and an old reporter.

Apparently, the interview had officially begun.

"All right," Geoffrey started. "First question. How long has the band been together?"

Darla decided to chime in. "Too long," she sneered.

I thought Nina was going to leap over the band to strangle the skinny bitch. "The band has been together for three years," she said, boring a hole into Darla's forehead with her silver eyes.

"But those years were bad," Mary Jane said. Her eyelids were so heavy she was struggling to keep them open. I predicted she'd nod off before the interview was over. "Real bad."

Athena jumped in. "We couldn't get a record deal. So we were playing a lot of bars and clubs. It was rough."

"And then your first single came out and it was an instant success for the band. Your song was already on the charts before the record deal."

"None of this was instant," Diego reminded the round-faced journalist. "We worked our asses off to get where we are today."

Nina's tight smile made her look like she was in pain. Did she have a spasm in her neck? "And they've loved every minute of it. Can't you tell?" she said.

"What about the name?" Geoffrey grinned, revealing a slight overbite. "Where did Sour Kitten come from?"

"That was Halo's idea. She just likes the words together. It doesn't conjure up a single image. It's noncommittal...like us. We're constantly changing," Athena explained.

"Change is good," Mary Jane echoed, staring at invisible specks of dust floating in the air around her chair. Maybe she saw something that the rest of us couldn't.

"Speaking of change," Nina said, "the band is now called the Jetsetters. It's in their new press kit, Geoffrey. I had a copy of it sent to your room earlier."

"I read it," he stated, "but I like Sour Kitten better. The Jetsetters sounds too pop to be punk."

"They were never officially Sour Kitten," Nina continued.

"And we were never officially punk either," Diego added. "Not even close."

Nina put a hand on Diego's shoulder, silencing him. "They started out as Broken Corners. Then the name was changed to the Jetsetters at the suggestion of their record label."

Geoffrey raised his squinty eyes and met Nina's. "I'm well aware of the history of the band," he said.

She could barely contain her rage. Her earlobes were purple. Her nostrils flared. She saw red and was ready to charge. "Look," she said, struggling to maintain her composure, "I know this interview is important. But they need to get upstairs and get some rest before their sold-out show tonight. We're leaving for L.A. in the morning."

"I still need to interview Halo Jet," he insisted.

"Don't you mean Brenda Stone?" Darla taunted. "Last time I saw her, she was passed out in an alley."

"She used to be your favorite singer," I reminded Darla. "You used to live and breathe for her."

Darla still avoided my eyes. She shrugged and said, "People change."

"Apparently they do," I shot back, "but not always for the better."

Nina stepped forward, and one of her four-inch heels barely missed Darla's foot. "I can arrange some time for you to meet with Halo," she said to Geoffrey.

"Where is Miss Jet?" he asked.

"Probably puking her guts up," Darla offered.

Nina spun around and raised her arm as if she were about to backhand Darla. I wished she would have. Instead, she lowered her arm just as fast as she'd lifted it, catching herself and grasping for self-control a millisecond before her temper got the best of her. Before she annihilated Darla Madrid with her bare hands. Instead, Nina closed her eyes for a few seconds and exhaled deeply, finding some form of peace within.

I smiled. Darla was closer to the truth than she realized. Halo was upstairs sleeping off a relapse. She'd been released from rehab earlier that morning. She stayed sober long enough to get to the airport. There, she wandered into the first bar she found and killed off nearly an entire bottle of tequila before stumbling onto the plane. Sitting in first class, she drank herself into unconsciousness, unaware the flight had landed in Las Vegas. Finally, two sympathetic flight attendants piled her into a wheelchair, pushed her into the terminal, and left her there to fend for herself, passed-out drunk. A security guard found her, retrieved Halo's cell phone from her purse, and answered it the fifth time a shrieking Nina called.

A half hour later, Halo arrived in front of the casino in a shuttle van, not sure where she was. Nina paid two hotel maids to stay with Halo, get her showered and cleaned up and pumped full of black coffee.

"Halo was feeling a little under the weather," she said to Geoffrey in a sugary voice that none of us bought. "I'll arrange for you to meet with her after the show tonight."

Mary Jane sat up, suddenly alert. "Can we go soon?" she asked. "I feel like nothing important is being said here."

"It's journalism, Mary Jane. It's their job to make things seem more important than they actually are," Diego said to his band mate. "But really, it's just a bunch of words on paper with little impact."

"You're quite a pessimist, aren't ya, Diego?" Geoffrey shot at him.

Finally, Darla acknowledged my presence. "That's not all he is," she said, and pointed at me. "Ask *him*."

I mouthed the words "fuck you" to Darla, who appeared shocked and insulted by my response. Her mouth even dropped open. I secretly wished Athena would've had one of her drumsticks on hand to silence the newly born monster once and for all.

"No, Geoffrey, I just don't like reporters," Diego said.

"Why's that?"

"Because they don't seem to like our music. I've read the early reviews of our new single. They're not taking us seriously."

Geoffrey smirked. "And with a name like the Jetsetters you expect to be taken seriously? You've only recorded one original song so far. It's a good one. I'll give you that. But the rest are all covers. The Yardbirds. Berlin. Concrete Blonde. Who in the hell *are* the Jetsetters? What is *your* sound?"

"Our music speaks for itself," Diego said.

"It does," Mary Jane agreed. She tilted back in her chair and put her arms behind her head. She looked up at the ceiling, at the twinkling of the chandeliers. "Lock yourself in a room and turn off the lights and put on some headphones and find a really good pillow. Then lie back, close your eyes, and enjoy the ride. If you do that with our music, you'll have an awesome time."

Athena tugged on the sleeve of Mary Jane's blouse. "Jesus, Mary Jane, get a grip."

Geoffrey leaned forward in his seat. "One last question, and it's the obvious one," he said. "Why make music? Why be in a band?"

Diego flashed his smile, cracked his knuckles, and answered with, "Why else? We wanna be fucking rock stars."

❖

I was surprised to find Diego waiting for me the minute I stepped out of the shower. I thought he was asleep on the king-sized bed, taking a power nap.

I knew we were pressed for time. According to the detailed schedule Nina had drilled into each of us after the interview with Geoffrey, the band needed to do a sound check and some radio promo spots, autograph some T-shirts for a giveaway, pose for some photos for local papers, and perform later that night to a sold-out crowd of nearly two thousand people.

"Hey," I said when he suddenly appeared in the doorway of the marble-tiled bathroom in a pair of white boxers and nothing else. Like our room, the bathroom was grand and impressive. I felt like I'd won something from a game show: a week-long stay at a fancy casino hotel. "You ready for the show tonight?"

I reached out and wiped a hand across the thick layer of steam covering the mirror above the double sinks. In the glass, I saw him appear behind me.

He started to kiss my neck. His lips brushed against my skin. I felt his hot breath. There was urgency in it. He reached around my body and pinched my nipples before trailing his fingertips down my stomach. I shuddered from the sensation. Before I realized what was happening, Diego ripped the bath towel away from my hips.

"Diego—" I started to say.

He reached inside his boxers, pulled out his hard cock, and bent me over the sink. I grabbed onto the smoothed edges of the marble counter. I closed my eyes when I felt him slide slowly inside me. A low moan tumbled out of me. It felt *that* good.

I could see him in the mirror, thrusting against me. His bangs fell into his eyes as he started to pump me as hard as he could. There was intensity on his beautiful unshaven face; a hot lust was burning in his expression.

"Fuck me," I begged, encouraging him to go even deeper.

Moments later, an orgasm rippled through his body. He collapsed on top of my back and whispered "I don't think I can live without you" into my damp skin.

CHAPTER EIGHTEEN

I don't really remember how Halo Jet and I became close friends, but our lives started to merge after the show that night in Las Vegas.

I was standing backstage in a green-tiled corridor, waiting for the band to finish their last song. The fluorescent lights above me flickered and twitched, reminding me of the hallway at my hometown high school. It felt like a hundred years had passed since I was that quiet, shy kid who rarely spoke from the back of the class, terrified if I opened my mouth everyone would discover the deep secret that I liked boys.

I noticed him at the opposite end of the hall. He was pacing back and forth outside of the dressing room door with Halo's name on it. He was holding a white envelope. He looked a few years older than me. He was taller, had an athletic build and shaggy brown hair. I wondered if he'd gotten lost on the way to a frat party.

Nina was on him like a mother tiger. They exchanged heated words. I strained to hear what they were saying, but the roar from the audience muted their conversation. By the flashes of anger on Nina's face and the college boy's insistence, I knew our surprise guest was also an uninvited one.

Mary Jane stumbled down the metal steps from the back of the stage. She reached for the railing to steady herself. She looked down at her glittery platform shoes and said, "Shit."

"Are you all right?" I asked.

"That was crazy, Justin," she said. I had no idea she even knew my name, or anyone else's, for that matter. "The audience—they knew the words to most of our songs. How did that happen?" She blinked at me a few times, perhaps considering I was personally responsible for teaching the entire audience the lyrics.

"Was it a good show?" I asked.

Athena appeared on the steps behind Mary Jane with a pair of drumsticks in her half-gloved hands. She was covered in sweat. "They've never screamed like that before," she said, wide-eyed and flushed. "Never."

"Where did they all come from?" Mary Jane asked Athena.

Their supercharged energy was contagious. I couldn't help smiling, especially when I saw Diego come down the stairs. He threw his arms around me and squeezed me tight. I felt the air pushed out of my lungs. "That was so fucking awesome! They loved us." He pulled away from me. "And I love you."

I touched his sweaty face. "I love you, too."

"For fuck's sake, take it upstairs to your room!" Halo appeared in a black glittery baby doll dress, fishnet stockings, and scarlet red heels. Her platinum-streaked auburn locks were pulled back into a slicked ponytail. She took each step carefully, as if it were a chore to even walk. She'd missed the sound check, the radio spots, the press. Nina had apologized on her behalf, explaining Halo had a touch of the flu and was saving up her energy to perform.

The two hotel maids, who'd been assigned the task of babysitting her, delivered Halo backstage less than a half an hour before the band was scheduled to go on. She'd sworn to each member of the band she was sobered up from her drunken journey, but I suspected otherwise. Somewhere along the way, she had to have stolen a sip or five from a bottle of something. Otherwise, she'd be the first woman I'd ever known who was permanently drunk.

"Well, that was fun," she deadpanned to her band members. "Wanna do it again tomorrow night...say...in Los Angeles?"

"You okay?" Athena asked her.

"Never better," she shot back. "I didn't puke onstage this time, so may I please be released early for my good behavior?"

"We're just worried about you," Mary Jane offered.

"Is that why you stuck me with Hortensia and Bitch Face? Those two wouldn't let me out of their sight. I got lectured in English, Spanish, *and* Russian about the badness of booze all fucking day long. Just the sound of their voices made me want to order a cocktail."

Nina suddenly appeared in our circle. "Halo," she said, with caution. "There's someone here to see you."

Halo shot her mother a look. "Cut the crap," she insisted. "Who is it? Who's here? And who's got a smoke for me?"

Nina swallowed before she spoke. "It's Roger."

Halo shook her head. "No," she said. "No...you tell that bastard to leave. I want nothing to do with him. Ever again."

"He's not taking no for an answer," Nina explained.

"Then do something. Call fucking security. You're the manager, Mom. Figure it out!"

"There's a lot of press here. If he makes a scene—"

"Fine!" Halo's eyes suddenly found me amongst the faces surrounding her. She grabbed me by the wrist. "Come with me."

I looked to Diego for help. "Go," he mouthed with a reassuring nod and smile.

Seconds later, Halo and I sailed into her dressing room, which was only half the size of my studio apartment back in Chicago. The room consisted of nothing more than a vanity table and mirror, a tan-colored plush leather sofa, and a mini-fridge. There was a sliding door in the far corner leading to a ridiculously small bathroom. Clearly, the Jetsetters hadn't made it to the top yet, despite being headliners for the night. I had spied much larger dressing rooms further down the hall. Given the fast track the band was on, I knew it was just a matter of time—probably weeks—before they reached a new level of success.

Halo leaned toward the lighted mirror. She seemed somewhat disgusted by her reflection. She swiped at specks of silver glitter on her cheeks. "Why would anybody want to buy anything from me?" she said aloud.

"Because you're amazing," I answered from where I sat on the incredibly comfortable sofa. I hadn't eaten much all day. I was worn out already, exhausted. I wanted to sleep. I wanted to be with Diego.

It's only the first night of the tour. You're never gonna make it.

Our eyes met in the glass. I wondered if Halo was about to cry. "No, I'm not," she said to both of us. "I never will be."

"That's bullshit and you know it," I said.

"You're wrong, lover boy."

"Am I? Then why are you here?"

She held my gaze. "What kind of a question is that?"

"I can't figure you out. Either you're incredibly ungrateful or you're telling the truth," I said. "You're an amazing performer."

She shook her head. I could see the tears filling her eyes. "No, I'm not. I wear slutty outfits and I can carry a tune. That hardly makes me brilliant."

"Then why do it? Why starve for three years and work your ass off if you hate it so much?"

Her eyes narrowed. "Are you interviewing me?"

"You have a chance right now that a million girls would kill for," I said.

"You don't think I know that?" she said. "I feel like an asshole every time I go on stage. I took someone else's spot."

"Then do something with it," I said. "Something that matters."

"Everyone's a sellout," she said. I gave her a look of disbelief. It was a lame excuse and she knew it. "It's true. In the beginning when people are hungry and desperate, they give a shit about the music they're making. Then along comes a record company and convinces them nothing they're doing is any good unless it can get on the radio."

"So? It's a business," I reminded her.

"So, maybe this is the wrong business for me," she said. "Maybe I'm not this kind of girl."

"Then what kind of girl are you?" I asked.

The expression on her face shifted. "Do you like pancakes?" she asked. "Do you think I'd make a good waitress?"

She turned suddenly toward the open doorway as if she sensed the presence of an intruder. Fury flooded her eyes.

"What are *you* doing here?" she asked the guy I assumed to be Roger. He took one step inside the dressing room. He was standing so close to me, I could see the dark hairs on his tanned knuckles.

Immediately, I wanted to leave. The space was too tight for the three of us to share comfortably, especially if I was about to witness a battle between them. I had no business being in there, being privy to their private words.

He stared at her with weary eyes and said, "You look like shit."

Halo sat down in a padded chair, still facing her reflection. In that moment, I thought she looked radiant. Granted, she was lit up by the strip of tiny bulbs surrounding the mirror, but there was a golden glow emanating from her like magic was seeping out of her pores. Her tone softened as she gazed at him. "I missed you, too."

"I saw the show tonight."

She locked eyes with him in the glass. "Half those songs were about you."

He grew tense. One of his knuckles twitched. "You're still angry?"

"Until the day you die," she said. "Any idea when that will be?"

"I hear you're going back to L.A. tomorrow."

Halo reached for a pack of cigarettes and a book of matches. She lit a smoke, took a drag, tilted her head back, and exhaled. She reminded me of a movie star from the '30s or '40s. She was glamorous, yet brokenhearted. A beautiful, intoxicating mixture of melodrama and misery. She was a living, breathing tragedy.

But she looked so great playing the role.

"Did you come here to throw me a going-away party?"

"The last time I saw you—"

Halo was on her feet at once. She pointed a finger in his direction, jabbing the air. I thought she might burn him with her cigarette. "The last time I saw *you*, I got my heart broken. What are you planning to do to me this time, Roger?"

He held out the envelope, presenting it to her. I noticed his fingers were shaking. "You asked me to write it all down. To put my feelings on paper."

She snatched the envelope out of his hand. "And?"

"And I did."

"Why are you here?"

"I told you—" He glanced in my direction and back to Halo. "Can we talk alone? In private?"

Awkward. I'll be going now.

"You worried my best friend might think less of you if he hears about the shitty things you've put me through?"

Wait...best friend? Me? When in the hell did Halo Jet and I become BFFs? Where was I when this love-fest started?

Roger shrugged and slid the tips of his fingers into the front pockets of his jeans. "Maybe," he answered.

That's your cue. This is none of your business, Justin. Time to go. Maybe you and Diego can hit an all-night buffet before heading back to the room.

I stood up to leave. Halo reached across Roger and shoved me back into the sofa. She grabbed a handful of her ex-boyfriend's Abercrombie & Fitch T-shirt. "He's more of a man than you'll ever be," she said. "Do you know what it does to me to see you, Roger? It rips me apart inside. Why did you come here?"

He actually looked scared of her. "I'm sorry."

She pushed herself off him, like he was a wall in a swimming pool. "It's a little late for apologies."

"I didn't mean to hurt you, Brenda."

She returned to her seat facing the mirror. "My name's Halo now."

"What?"

"Halo. *Halo!* H-A-L-O."

He shook his head. "Jesus Christ. What have they done to you?"

"Nothing you didn't do."

"You can't blame me for walking away. This isn't the life I want. I told you that. I explained it to you. I'm an architect. All this I-wanna-be-a-rock-star bullshit is just too much for me to handle."

"It wouldn't have mattered. I could've been a librarian or a waitress and I still would've been too much for you. We both know why you broke up with me. It's because your mother's an uptight bitch and she hates me."

His mother sounds a lot like your own mother, Halo. Does everyone's mother hate you? Mine probably would. She'd be nice to your face, though.

Roger didn't argue. I knew what Halo had said was true. Just by looking at him, I could tell he was the wrong guy for her. He was too conservative. Too Republican. Too normal.

"I just wanted to give you the letter," he explained.

She took another drag. "Well, you did," she said. "Now go build something and jump off it. I'm redesigning my life, and you're not in it."

He genuinely looked hurt. "Maybe someday we can be friends."

She shook her head. "I'm not a very good friend. I either fuck 'em or puke on 'em."

"I need to go," he decided. "I'm leaving now." He turned and started to walk out of the room.

She rose to her feet again. She stopped him with her voice. "You already left me once."

"I hope someday we can put all of this behind us. You don't need me, Brenda. You never did."

She stepped toward him. He didn't flinch. "You're fucking wrong. I needed you more than I needed anything. Instead, I lost you and now they say I'm gonna have a hit song. You served your purpose, Roger," she said. "Now, get the fuck out and let me die in misery, okay?"

He reached out as if he wanted to touch her, but she stopped him with the cold anger in her eyes.

"Just know I'll always care about you." With that, Roger turned and walked away.

Halo stepped out into the corridor. Apparently, she was determined to have the last word.

"Yeah…well, fuck you, *Roger*! Fuck you and your pathetic buildings made of crap and broken fucking promises! I'm gonna write another song about you and tell the entire world what a cocksucker you are! It'll be a number one hit and every woman in America will know my pain! And every time I sing it, I'll dedicate it to you…you *fucker*!"

❖

Halo's interview with Geoffrey Cole seemed more like an interrogation. The lead singer was sitting in an oversized red leather chair beneath the harsh glare of a stark overhead lamp. We were stuffed inside a room no bigger than a closet, not far from the lobby of the hotel and the main floor of the casino. I wondered if this is where people who cheated at poker tables were brought and tortured. Through the thin walls, I could hear the clanging of slot machines and a lounge singer's horrible rendition of Charlene's "I've Never Been to Me."

Geoffrey reeked like cheap aftershave. My eyes burned. There was very little air in the room. I was more than ready to leave and return to my room, where I knew Diego was waiting for me.

Hopefully naked.

Halo had insisted I come with her to the interview. She told Nina she couldn't get through it without me at her side.

I was quickly discovering that Halo always got her way. No one seemed to have the energy, or the nerve, to challenge her.

Geoffrey launched his first question. "Forgive me for saying this, but you seem a lot calmer sitting here than when you're performing on stage. Any reason why?"

I thought she was going to punch him in the face. "Calm?" she said. "You think I'm calm, Geoffrey?"

She was teasing him, taunting him to push her over the edge and detonate. She would explode all over him and wipe the room with his ass.

"You already have a reputation for being a bit…wild. Where does the anger come from?"

"I'm a woman in the music industry who's had her heart broken," she said. "What do you expect?"

"Do you hate the world?"

She nodded. "Sometimes."

"Do you hate men?"

She locked eyes with him. "Only if I date them."

"What about your family? I know who your mother is, but where's your father?"

She looked away. "No comment."

He raised an eyebrow. "No?"

"My music is my family. The band. The kids who come to the shows—that's my family. We're all related because we want the same thing: to feel loved."

"There are rumors about you performing drunk on stage in Paris, screaming profanities at a record producer, and even a suicide attempt a year ago. Do you feel guilty about your behavior?"

"Hey," she said, "I never asked to be a role model. When we

first started the band, I was mixed up in some pretty hard-core stuff. I gave it all up when things started to go my way."

"And now?" he asked. "Are things going your way?"

She leaned forward. She glanced down at his mouth, then back up to his eyes. "You tell me."

"I'd say so. A hit single. Sold-out shows across the country. A highly anticipated debut album in the works."

"It all sounds yummy to me." She grinned. "If I wasn't on the verge of major success, Geoffrey, I'd be interviewing you instead."

He snorted and blushed. "I'm afraid I'm not as…interesting… as you are."

Her smile and kindness faded. "I'm sure that girl you brought with you to Las Vegas would disagree."

"Darla?" he said, surprised.

"The one who looks like an escort," Halo said. "Are you paying her well?"

"My private life is—"

"Pathetic," Halo completed. "Look at her, Geoffrey. Ask yourself, what is a girl like *that* doing with a piece of shit like *you*?"

"Have *you* ever been in love?" he threw at her.

"Once," she said. "But it'll never happen again. I gave it up when I quit drugs. Both of them left me kind of numb."

"I'm not surprised," he said. "Girls like you don't usually have serious boyfriends."

"Girls like me usually steal other people's boyfriends," she explained. "Because we can."

"Where do you see yourself in five years, Halo?"

"Under a tree," she said. "I'm sure you'll come visit me. To pay your…respects."

"Do you suffer from depression?"

She shook her head. "No, but depression suffers me. It will probably become my trademark."

Geoffrey Cole gave Halo a genuine look of concern. "Why do you think that is?"

Halo leaned back in the comfy-looking leather chair. She looked over at me. I saw the haunted sorrow floating in her eyes, the evidence of the crushed hopes Roger had left behind. For a brief second, I caught a quick glimpse of the girl Halo once was. I saw a young Brenda, a girl with love and hope illuminating her pure heart with a beautiful glow. Before the boys. Before the band. Her world was once innocent. There was a shred of it still left inside her. You could see it, but you had to look closely.

Halo wiped the corners of her eyes with the back of her hand. She swallowed as if her emotions were starting to choke her and answered, "Because no one else can suffer as beautifully as I can."

Chapter Nineteen

I was getting worried about you," Diego said when I walked into the hotel room. He was sitting on the edge of our bed with an acoustic guitar in his hands and a bottle of beer within reach. He was shirtless and barefoot, wearing only a pair of black basketball shorts. I wanted to push him back onto the bed and lick every inch of his delicious, warm skin. I fought my urges off and focused on his words. "I finished writing the song about us. The one I started in Chicago. You wanna hear it?"

I moved to him. I kissed the barbed-wire tattoo that circled his left arm. I ran a hand through his messy, thick hair. I felt a pang of lust start to grow between my legs. I pulled away from him quickly. "I would love to," I answered.

I sank into a floral patterned love seat near the floor-to-ceiling window and watched Diego from across the room, where I wouldn't be tempted to rip off his clothes and straddle his body.

He strummed the guitar, cleared his throat, and started to sing. His voice was smooth and gentle. The song was soft and sweet. It reminded me of a lullaby. But then he launched into the chorus and the song shifted into a desperate plea for love.

"Don't walk away from me. Justin, can't you see? My heart has been…crushed. I searched the world for you. But from our kiss, I knew. You are my sudden…hush. I love our silent stares, our teases and dares, and the softness of your…touch. Some say our love is wrong. So I wrote this song. 'Cuz I'm in love with you so much."

Maybe it was the lyrics. Or the intensity in Diego's cinnamon-colored eyes. Or the fragile cracks of emotion in his voice. But by the time he finished the song, I was on the verge of tears. I was more in love with Diego Delgado than ever. And this terrified me.

I wasn't expecting someone like him to ever appear in my life. Our relationship had never been on my radar, not even on the secret wish lists I sometimes wrote out on the back of the coffee-colored napkins at Clouds. That afternoon when he'd walked in with the Broken Corners concert poster in his hands felt like a million years ago. So much had happened since. Thinking about it made me feel like I'd just sprinted a five-hundred-yard dash in a matter of seconds.

Diego leaned his guitar against the nightstand, looked at me, and asked, "What did you think?"

I blinked back my tears and managed to get out, "Diego… wow."

He came to me then. He moved slowly across the carpet, crawling on all fours like a cat. He was seducing me with each slow, fluid motion he made. He reached me and slid a hand from my ankle up my calf, and tickled the inside of my thigh with his fingers. He was kneeling at my feet, looking up and seeking approval. I touched his beautiful face, his tender lips. "I love you, Justin," he said, not once breaking our gaze. "I meant every word of that song."

"I love you, too," I replied. "I wouldn't be here in Las Vegas with you if I didn't."

He turned his face and kissed my palm. He closed his eyes and placed his head in my lap. I stroked his hair, sliding my fingers through strands of hot magenta, bright blue, jet black. I glanced to the window and caught a breathtaking glimpse of the Las Vegas Strip. The city seemed magical to me. The lights were twinkling for us, like stars. Like the illuminated souls of other lovers who had found each other, too.

Diego's words kissed the outer ridges of my heart. "I don't think I could ever live without you, Justin."

A couple of hours later we were curled up together in the dark.

We'd taken a shower together. Made love. Ordered room service. Watched *Like Water for Chocolate* on cable. Talked about the tour, the band, the cities we would travel to in the weeks to come. How angry Diego still was with Nina. How worried he was about Halo.

After a while, we both fell into a blanket of silence.

I could see the late night Nevada sky through a crack in the golden drapes. I stared at the cloudless span of infinite space. It looked like the horizon never ended.

I knew I'd made the right choice by agreeing to join Diego on the road. As crazy as we were about one another, I wasn't entirely confident that our new relationship would've survived being separated for five weeks.

Yet I was already missing the familiarity of Chicago. The rumble of the "L" train. The majesty of Lake Michigan. My apartment. My walk to work each morning. My regular customers at Clouds. My daily conversations with Starsky. All of these things were a part of my everyday life. I felt my world was disappearing—and fast—with each moment I spent away from it. As much I liked each member of the band, I wasn't sure I belonged in their circle. I still felt like an outsider.

The sound of Diego's voice surprised me because I thought he'd fallen asleep. His soft words cut through the dark and tiptoed across my bare skin. "I miss my mom," he said.

I felt my body tense. I wasn't ready for this—his grief.

What do I say to him? What's the right thing to do in this moment? Fuck.

"Come here," I urged. I pulled him toward me and he slid

into my arms. I kissed the back of his neck and whispered, "I know you do."

"I hate it," he said. His voice cracked. His body began to shake with emotion. It was then I realized Diego was crying. In my arms. "I don't want her to be gone."

I tightened my grip on Diego, reassuring him that no matter what, I wasn't going anywhere.

Chapter Twenty

All hell broke loose in Los Angeles.

We were there for less than forty-eight hours but each second was filled with conflict, confrontation, and career-changing decisions.

I maintained a low profile. I kept my mouth shut. I hung back, observed, and only offered my opinion when asked. I did my best to stay out of everyone's way, including Diego's.

Like Las Vegas, I'd never been to Los Angeles before. I was in complete awe of my surroundings. Everyone I met, saw, spoke to—even strangers at a place I later discovered called the Coffee Bean and Tea Leaf—looked like they'd leapt off the pages of an airbrushed magazine ad. I felt incredibly self-conscious, uncool, and awkwardly out of place.

The sights and sounds and smells of Los Angeles were overwhelming. I loved the beautiful shore. The winding canyon roads. The perfect temperature.

Yet I knew L.A. would never be home.

I began to plan a conversation in my mind in which I would have to tell Diego I could never live in this place, this planet of pretty, pretentious people.

Chicago was home to me.

Athena drove us from Las Vegas to L.A. in a cramped passenger van. Nina spent the entire five hours on her cell phone shrieking at anyone she could get on the line. Mary Jane passed out with her headphones on and drooled all over her pink tank top. Diego and I occupied ourselves with scribbled games of Tic-tac-toe and Hangman and constant flirting. Halo rctreated from the world and delved into the pages of a fashion magazine.

After dropping Mary Jane off at her apartment in North Hollywood, delivering Nina to her office on Fairfax Avenue, and helping Halo up to her third-floor apartment in Santa Monica, Athena headed south to a place called Redondo Beach. She owned an oceanfront Spanish-styled condo there, courtesy of the wealthy parents she referred to as Chuck and Connie, or "the rich bastards." Diego was her roommate, so this was the place he called home.

Veronica Marie was already there when we arrived. We stood in the doorway, sweaty and miserable, clutching our suitcases and discarded remnants from fast-food drive-thrus. I wanted a shower. A home-cooked meal. A good night's sleep.

The Brazilian supermodel was posed on the sun-drenched terrace, staring down at the swimming pool. She was wearing a canary yellow bikini, a white sarong around her hips, and strapped high heels. She had an oversized drink in her hand that I assumed was a daiquiri. On her head was an enormous—and perfectly angled—sun hat. She looked like she'd stepped off the set of a modern version of *Dynasty*. I expected Joan Collins to jump out at any moment and exclaim, "Veronica Marie, I've been searching for you everywhere! I'm your *real* mother, darling."

Instead, Veronica Marie launched into a tirade. This pissed me off because I really needed to pee.

"This is bullshit! Athena, I'm not putting up with this anymore!"

Athena let out a deep sigh. "What are you talking about?"

Veronica Marie stood in front of us with a haughty hand on her bony hip. "I checked the messages on your answering machine when I got here."

I could see anger flash in Athena's eyes. I prayed she didn't have a temper. "You did *what*?"

"Who in the hell is Rebel Crawford? Another one of your groupies?"

Oh, shit. Not again.

"Jesus Christ…Veronica, you're making a big deal out of nothing."

Veronica Marie turned on her heels and stormed back onto the terrace. Maybe she was determined to give all those hanging out at the pool an afternoon performance. I waited for her to break out with an a capella version of "Don't Cry for Me Argentina."

"Don't think I'm stupid just because I'm a model," she said. "I went to college, I'll have you know. I speak four languages."

"Yeah and she's a bitch in all of them," Diego whispered in my ear.

I bit the inside of my cheek to prevent a roar of laughter.

Athena joined her on the terrace. "I never said you were stupid. You need to calm down. You're starting to get on my nerves."

"Oh *really*?!"

"Look, things have been great between us. It's been wonderful."

"Fuck wonderful and fuck you."

"Diego," I said, "where's the bathroom?"

"First door on the left," he said, gesturing to a hallway near the large kitchen.

The condo was immaculate. I wondered if Athena paid someone to clean every inch of it on the hour. Nothing was out of place. Everything was color coordinated. Very plush. Very chic. Very expensive.

When I grow up, may I please be a rich lesbian drummer in a rock 'n' roll band? Or at least have a trust fund with my name on it?

Even in the bathroom, I could still hear every word of Veronica Marie's over-the-top outburst.

"Come inside, Veronica. I'll fix you another drink."

"Go to hell!"

"Baby, please. I brought you something from Vegas."

"I don't want it. Give it to *her*."

"Veronica, can't you try to be nice for one second? We're in the middle of a tour. I've been driving since seven this morning. I'm really tired. We have a show tonight and we're recording all day tomorrow."

"Are you calling me a *bitch*?"

Okay. Clearly Veronica Marie is insane. Now the crazy woman is hearing things.

"I never said that."

I washed my hands with soap that smelled like tangerines and rushed back to the living room. Diego was sitting on a comfortable-looking L-shaped white sofa. I joined him.

"This is getting good," he said.

"I know exactly why you asked me out…for the *publicity*!" Veronica Marie insisted. "Tell me I'm wrong."

"That's not true and you know it. You're in the closet. Everyone thinks you're straight."

Veronica Marie stormed back into the house. Athena reluctantly followed.

Veronica Marie reached for something on the kitchen counter. It was one of those sleazy tabloids found at the checkout line in any supermarket. She flipped it open, gouged a black-and-white photo with her claw-like fingernail, and shouted to Athena, "Not anymore!"

Athena took the gossip rag from her and said, "Oh…fuck."

Veronica Marie gulped back the rest of her daiquiri, and I wondered if supermodels were immune to a brain freeze. Then I started craving a piña colada Slurpee from 7-Eleven.

And a bag of Funyuns.

Do they even have 7-Elevens in L.A.?

"You don't even know me, Athena. You know my face, my body, what I look like on the cover of a magazine. But you don't give a damn about who I really am."

I wanted to ask Veronica Marie if she'd ever auditioned for a role on *The Bold and the Beautiful* but resisted.

"Will you stop it?" Athena said. "My God, you're so full of yourself."

"You're one to talk, with your sixteen-year-old groupies."

"She's nineteen!"

"It's disgusting how you treat women."

"Well, if you don't like it, then you can leave."

Veronica Marie stood for a moment, majestic in her fury, then went to a coat closet near the front door. She wheeled out two suitcases, already packed.

Surprise! She's been ready to go for hours.

"Fine, then. I'm leaving," she told Athena. "But don't *ever* expect me to come back." She scanned the room, seething at each of us. "None of you will *ever* see me again…*Ever*!"

She tried to make a dramatic exit but the door to the condo smacked her in the back of her head and nearly caused her to slip down the cement steps to the gardenia-filled courtyard below. "Son of a bitch!" she bellowed.

Apparently, she had more to say. Once her suitcases, her Coco Chanel purse, and her empty daiquiri glass were safely out of the apartment, she posted herself in the open doorway and declared, as only a true diva could: "There's just one more thing. I swear to God, if you trash me to the press, I'll ruin you and your bubblegum career, you got that? Now if you'll excuse me, Athena, I need to find myself a real woman."

Of course, she slammed the door as hard as she could. A picture fell off the wall and the glass frame shattered.

Diego turned to me and asked, "Um…would you like to go for a walk on the beach?"

I nodded and replied with a smile, "I'd love to."

❖

Athena was concerned about the merchandise table and, for once, Nina was nowhere in sight to do her job. Athena approached me backstage—just minutes before the Jetsetters were scheduled to go on—and asked me if I'd go to the front lobby of the venue to confirm their souvenir T-shirts and posters had been properly set up by two female roadies.

There I overheard a conversation between the two young women in question. While they opened boxes of T-shirts and tacked up posters and price tags, they exchanged words.

"Halo Jet is a drunk bitch," said the overweight one with a bad dye job and blotchy skin. She was wearing a pair of faded overalls begging to be put out of their misery.

"And she can't sing," agreed her dark-haired slender friend, who was wearing a denim miniskirt, a green halter, and a lopsided ponytail. She reminded me of Popeye's girlfriend Olive Oyl.

"I can't believe the way she talks to people," the chubby-faced blonde continued. "She thinks she's so cool."

"How do you think she became famous?" her friend asked.

"Duh. How else?"

Olive Oyl's doppelganger let out a gasp, followed by: "Are you serious?"

"I swear to God. Mindy in the sound booth told me Halo slept with three record execs to get a contract."

"She really did that?"

Out of the corner of my eye, I saw her: Nina was lurking in the background, listening to their every word. *Waiting.*

"Yes," the blonde said, "but her career's already a mess. It'll be over before it even started. I mean, look at her." She pointed at one of the posters. "Have you ever seen an uglier singer? She looks like a slut."

The brunette snorted and choked on her laugh. "Do you still wish we were famous?" she asked her cohort.

"Hell yes," she said. "It's better than being some lame-ass roadie with this piece-of-shit band."

"You don't like the Jetsetters?" the skinny twig asked in mock shock.

"It's trash. Besides, Athena is the only talented person in the band."

"Oh, I know. You're *so* right. What do you think about the rest of them?"

Yes, tell us. Right before you get destroyed.

Nina was pacing, fired up. Enraged. These two dumbasses would never even know what hit them.

"Mary Jane's always doped up and crying her eyes out to her mother on the phone. Athena's getting on with every groupie she can find. Halo is an alcoholic schizo. And I heard their manager was born in hell."

"What about Diego?"

Yes...what about Diego?

"He's the only one with any hope. But that's just because he's pretty. He can't play a guitar to save his life."

Take it back, bitch.

Apparently, the blonde hadn't said enough about Diego. "I also hear he's a fag."

Her friend shook her head and said, "Wow...what a shame."

"I kinda figured he was," she said. "Lord knows he wouldn't wanna fuck Halo. Nobody would."

That's when it happened.

Nina Grey stepped forward. She looked like a parent chaperone for a fourth-grade field trip. She should've been waiting in a car-pool line in front of a school somewhere to take her twins to after-school soccer practice and swimming lessons. In her matronly white ruffled blouse and navy blue polyester slacks, she seemed completely out of place at a rock concert.

But then she opened her mouth.

"I don't know who you two nasty little *bitches* think you are, but you're talking about my daughter," she began. "Now shut your mouths for a second and listen to me or else I'm gonna hafta kick your fucking teeth in."

I stood there and listened to her unleash her wrath on them, reducing them to a puddle of suicidal tears. They couldn't get away from her fast enough. Once she'd spewed her last profanity at them, they scurried off to seek shelter in the ladies' room like frightened rats.

When they were gone, Nina turned to me. "Don't ever breathe a word of that to anyone," she instructed me.

"I'm surprised," I said. "I never figured you for the maternal type."

"Then you don't really know me," she said, before walking away.

❖

Minutes after their performance ended that night, panic set in.

As I'd done in Las Vegas, I waited backstage for each member of the band to make his or her exit. We were in an old nightclub from the 1940s, converted a few years ago into a concert hall. The backstage area was dimly lit and creepy. It was in the basement and it felt haunted. I wondered how many ghosts of dead rock stars were roaming the maze of hallways that snaked their way beneath the wooden dance floor and stage above.

Halo came off first, more pumped up and energized than I'd ever seen her.

"Good show?" I asked.

"Awesome!" she enthused.

"You must be sober," I cracked.

"For once," she answered with a smile. "I've got something to do, lover boy. So tell everyone to leave me alone for a while."

I nodded, keeping my eyes glued to the stage door, waiting anxiously for Diego to appear.

Behind me, I heard the door of Halo's dressing room shut and lock. A tiny flicker of concern ignited inside me.

She's up to something.

I shook off the thought when Athena and Mary Jane entered the backstage area, arm in arm. Mary Jane didn't look well.

"Is everything okay?" I asked.

"I made her promise me and look what she did," Athena said, trying to hold up an almost unconscious Mary Jane. "Help me get her to her dressing room."

I slid my arm around Mary Jane's bone-thin waist and assisted Athena in maneuvering the bass player to an overstuffed, drab old sofa in her chilly dressing room. Mary Jane floated from our arms like a piece of paper. She was a letter being delivered via airmail, landing on the lumpy couch.

"What's the matter with her?" I asked.

"I'm not sure. Where's her purse?"

I scanned the room. "I don't know. I don't see it."

"Help me find it," Athena insisted.

The room was bare, other than a crystal vase with a single white carnation in it. It was a token of appreciation, given to each member of the band from the club's owner. "It's not here, Athena."

"Well, did someone steal it? It's gotta be here."

"Look," I said. "There's nothing in this room." I poked my head into the bathroom and the small shower stall. "Or in here."

"What the fuck…"

Diego appeared in the doorway then, sweaty and breathless. "What's going on?" His eyes moved to the sofa where Mary Jane was now passed out cold. "Oh, shit. Is she all right?"

Athena bent over Mary Jane and slapped her face lightly. "Mary Jane?" she said, loud. "What did you take? Where's your purse?"

"Where's Nina?" Diego asked. "We should call someone."

"Athena, she doesn't look good," I said.

Nina shoved her way into the room. “She’s fine.”

“No, she’s not,” Athena said.

“I gave her a couple of Valium before thc show,” Nina explained.

“Why would you do that?” Diego asked.

“She didn’t want any of you to know this, but she’s been off the pills since Europe.”

“So then why did you give her one?” Athena said.

“She was too tense. She’s got a horrible case of stage fright. That’s why she took them to begin with.”

“No,” Diego corrected her. “Mary Jane takes them because she’s an addict.”

“Listen, I know for a fact she didn’t take them. I put her purse in Halo’s dressing room.”

Then it hit me.

“Did Halo know about that?” I asked “About the purse and the pills?”

“Yes,” Nina explained. “Actually, it was her idea.”

Athena caught the fear in my eyes. “Where’s Halo?”

“She said she had something to do,” I explained. “She told me she wanted to be left alone.”

“Oh God, not again,” Nina said, turning away from us and racing down the hall. We followed at her heels, tripping over each other.

Nina reached the dressing room door first. She turned the knob. It was locked. She pounded on the door with her fists. “Brenda, open this door right this second! I’m your mother and you’re gonna listen to me!”

Athena shoved her out of the way. “That’s never gonna work, Nina,” she said.

“You got any better ideas?” Nina threw back at her.

“As a matter of fact, I do.” Athena stepped back, raised one of her heavy black combat boots, and rammed it into the door. Hinges and screws popped off of the frame. The door burst open wide.

"Where is she?" I heard Diego say.

I peered inside. The dressing room was empty.

Athena grabbed Mary Jane's pink glittery purse from the lit up vanity table. She flipped it over and dumped out its contents. Among other things, five pill bottles tumbled out, slid off the table, hit the floor, and rolled around our feet.

The bottles were empty.

"My God, did she take them all?" Nina said.

"Where in the fuck *is* she?" Athena added.

Our attention collectively moved to the corner of the room, to the closed bathroom door. As if to answer our question, we heard the sound of a toilet flushing. Seconds later, the door clicked, opened, and out walked Halo. We all breathed a sigh of relief in unison.

Halo looked at us. Then, she looked at the door.

"What in the fuck did you guys do?" she asked. "You all look guilty."

"Where's the pills?" Athena demanded, shaking Mary Jane's purse in front of Halo's face.

"Jesus Christ," she said, "calm down. I got rid of 'em. I flushed 'em down the toilet. Every single one of those fuckers is gone."

"Why would you do something like that?" Nina asked.

"Because I care about Mary Jane," she said. "Is that so difficult to believe?"

"Yes," Nina said with a nod, "it is."

Halo sat down at the vanity table. She reached out to the stem of the white carnation and slipped it out of the crystal vase. I saw drops of water fall from the bottom tip of the flower onto her black and metallic silver baby-doll dress. She closed her eyes, brought the flower to her nose, and smelled the sweet petals. "God, I love white carnations," she said.

"What's the matter with you?" Nina asked. "Are you on something now?"

"She's sober," I said in her defense.

“Lover boy’s right,” she said, tossing me a wink. “Fortunately, I didn’t get forced to take one of my mother’s Valiums. You used to love to give them to me…remember, Mom?”

“Now isn’t the time for this, Brenda.”

“I would appreciate it if you would address me by my professional name. Since you get twenty percent of everything I make, you owe me that much. My name is Halo Jet. And you can’t deny the diet pills you shoved down my throat when I was twelve for the beauty pageants you made me compete in. The tranquilizers when I tried to fight you. Or what about the two weeks you locked me up in that mental hospital and you told all of your friends I was away teaching dance classes at a summer camp for children with leukemia?”

Diego locked eyes with his manager. “My God, Nina…you did that?”

Halo smirked and rubbed the flower against her chin. “I can’t make this shit up.”

“This isn’t the time or the place,” Nina huffed.

“You’re a lousy manager,” Halo told her, “and you’re an even worse mother.”

“I’ve only wanted the best for you,” she replied. “Just like any parent would.”

“Well, I don’t think you’ll be winning any Mother of the Year awards anytime soon,” Halo said.

She stood up. She looked at me. “Hey, lover boy, will you hand me my sweater and my purse? They’re probably on the floor somewhere, since they were hanging on the back of the door before you maniacs decided to break it down.”

I found her beaded bag and her white cashmere button-up sweater and handed them to her.

“I’m leaving now,” she said to us, “but before I go, there’s something you should probably know.”

We were hanging on her every word. Her charisma was so powerful, none of us could take our eyes off of her. We were riveted by every movement she made, each breath she took. I understood the meaning of the phrase *star quality*. Halo Jet not only possessed it, she was the epitome of it.

Maybe that's why I was so shocked by what she said next.

"As of this moment," she began, "I am no longer a member of this band. I quit. I resign. I'm out."

"What?" Athena said. "What the fuck are you talking about?"

"I'll be working at a restaurant starting next week," Halo said.

"The hell you are," Nina protested.

"It's my choice," Halo insisted, locking eyes with her mother. "My mind is made up. The album hasn't been recorded yet. There's still time. Go find another girl singer. I'm staying here in Los Angeles. Just like Johnette sings, I'm still in Hollywood."

"You're quitting the band to become a waitress?" Athena said. "This is unbelievable."

"Are you out of your fucking mind?" Nina roared.

Halo shrugged and simply said, "Pancakes. I love pancakes."

"Then we'll buy you some," Diego offered. "We'll take you to IHOP whenever you want. Nina can ask them to sponsor the whole fucking tour for you."

"You're sweet, Diego," she said. "Stay that way."

"You're just gonna leave, Brenda?" Athena asked. "Just like that? After everything?"

"You guys will make it without me. I know you will."

"Are you sure about this?" I asked her. "Is that what you really want?"

"I took what little money I've earned so far with this band and I went and bought myself a restaurant. A little pancake house. You should come and see it sometime. It's by the beach."

With that, Halo walked out of the dressing room. Nina,

Diego, Athena, and I scrambled into the hallway to catch our last glimpse of the former queen.

We were there just in timc to watch her dramatic exit.

Halo pushed open the emergency exit door and set off the alarm.

CHAPTER TWENTY-ONE

The next morning, Athena, Diego, and I arrived at the Geneva Recording Studios on Sunset Boulevard. The small bungalow styled building seemed quaint, almost like an ivy-covered cottage from a fairy tale.

We stood in the claustrophobic lobby, surrounded by wood-paneled walls covered with framed autographed photos of famous singers who'd recorded there. From the lobby, a narrow hallway led to the actual studios. From one of them, Mary Jane emerged with her pink bass guitar strapped around her neck. Her white-blond hair was pulled back into a loose ponytail. She was wearing gym shorts, flip-flops, and a tank top. She looked rested, ready to work.

"Hi, guys," she said with a smile.

Who is this person? She's actually alert and aware of what's happening in the universe.

Nina stepped in front of Mary Jane, intercepting her friendliness and replacing it with the icy glare in her gray eyes. She was wearing blue jeans, a sequined green Christmas sweatshirt, and miniature wreaths for earrings. "The three of you are late," she grumbled. She turned to me and added, "Including *you*."

"The 405 was insane," Athena explained, her car keys still in hand. "I got us here as fast as I could, Nina. We live in Redondo… remember?"

Diego hadn't said much to Athena and me all morning or last night. He'd retreated from the world and was deep in thought. His body was tense. His mood was dark. I let him have his space. I knew it was just a matter of time before he imploded.

"I've been on the phone all morning with the record label and our attorneys," Nina began. "We have a contract and we have to honor it. Studio time has been booked. Promotional appearances have been planned. Your first single is flying up the charts."

"What exactly are you saying?" Diego asked.

"I'm saying the band has to go on…with or without my daughter. We have an album to deliver. I say we get started on it right away."

"Are you still our manager?" Athena asked. "I thought…I figured…"

"I'm not quitting just because Halo did," she informed us. "I'm not running off to the nearest pancake house like some nut job. I see the potential here."

"Is it because of the money we're making?" Diego asked. "The money we stand to make? We're not a band anymore. We're a product. That's all we've ever been to you."

"Hey, Athena asked me to do this, to be here," Nina reminded him. "I didn't want to take this job. I was perfectly happy living my life."

"I figured it was a good idea at the time, Nina," she said. "You're the only one who can reel Halo in and keep a handle on her. But she's gone now."

"And we're still a band," Mary Jane chimed in.

"Don't think for a second you can toss me out," Nina warned, directing most of her words to Diego. "Just like you, I'm under contract. And I'm not going *anywhere*. Now…we have some studio time booked this morning. We have a flight to catch to New York tomorrow. The three of you need to focus on recording some tracks today. Let me handle the lead singer issue."

"What issue are you talking about?" Diego pushed.

"Obviously we need a new lead singer."

"Replace Halo? Just like that?" he snapped.

"You got any better ideas? I gotta work fast because the band has been booked on a late-night talk show tomorrow. You can thank me later."

"For what?" Diego asked. "For having no respect for us?"

"For making shit happen for the three of you. Before I came along you were busking down at the Third Street Promenade."

"I'm beginning to think maybe that life wasn't so bad," he said. "Maybe Halo was right."

"Don't threaten me, Diego," Nina said, holding an index finger up for emphasis.

"Or what?" he yelled. "You're going to forget to tell me that someone else died?"

Nina folded her arms across her chest. "I did what I had to do."

"And so did your daughter. And so will I. I don't give a fuck about being famous!"

"Blame me for everything if it's easier," she said. "Go on. I can take it."

"I'll never forgive you for the two days you waited to tell me about my mother. I should've been there, Nina. Not in some bar in Europe performing to a bunch of drunk assholes."

"I did it because I care about this band."

His voice filled every inch of the space around us. "You did it for the money!"

Diego turned and shoved the glass door open with such force, I almost expected it to shatter. He stepped out onto Sunset Boulevard and started to walk away.

Nina looked at me. "Can you please do something about him?"

"What do you want me to do?"

"He's your boyfriend, for fuck's sake. Go stop him for making the biggest mistake of his life." Nina turned away from us and stormed off to one of the studios, slamming the door shut behind her.

"Come on," Athena said to me. "I'll go with you."

Mary Jane blinked a few times. "Um…Athena? What should I do?"

"Meditate," she suggested.

❖

"Everything's a mess and I don't know how to fix it," Athena confided while we walked down Sunset Boulevard, searching for Diego. Even though it was December, it felt like a summer day. "None of this was supposed to happen."

"What do you want to do, Athena?" I asked. "Do you want to walk away from this?"

"Fuck no," she said. "I've worked my ass off, Justin. I've invested everything I've got into this band. I'm not just talking about cash from those rich bastards. This band is my life."

"Can you guys survive without Halo?"

She stopped suddenly in her steps. I did the same. We turned to face each other. "That's what I wanted to talk to you about."

"Me?" I said. "About what?"

"About this whole lead singer issue," she said. "I have an idea, but it can't happen without you. I need your help."

"Tell me what you want me to do."

❖

We found Diego sitting at a sidewalk table outside of a place called the Coffee Bean and Tea Leaf. He looked up when he saw us approaching. I glanced down at his left hand and noticed he was holding his father's dog tags.

"Look, I'm sorry," he began. "I'm sorry, Athena, because I know what you've done to make this band happen." He turned to me. "And I'm sorry I dragged you into this craziness."

"I'm here because I want to be here," I reminded him. "And because I love you."

Athena gave him a playful punch in the shoulder. "And I'm here because I'm a pissed-off dyke drummer and I need my guitar player and my best friend to get back to work so we can make some beautiful noise together."

"But how?" he asked.

"We've come up with a solution," I said, as I'd promised Athena just moments ago that I would.

I breathed in deep. The smell of coffee permeating the air made me incredibly homesick. I missed Starsky. And Hutch. And Clouds. And Chicago. I missed standing behind the espresso machine and making an outstanding cappuccino. I missed my life.

I need an iced chai tea latte. And some peace of mind, please. And for my boyfriend to think Athena's plan is a brilliant one. Because it is.

Diego looked to both of us for an explanation. "Well," he said, "what's your idea?"

"I don't think we need a new lead singer," Athena offered.

He looked at her like she was insane. "How is that even possible?"

I sat down in an empty chair beside him. I placed my hand over his, looked him in the eyes, and said, "You should be the lead singer of the Jetsetters."

CHAPTER TWENTY-TWO

Diego hated the idea. He insisted he was a guitar player, not a singer. He didn't crave attention from the public or the media. He didn't want to be in the center of the spotlight.

He just wanted to play guitar.

However, he did agree to return to the studios—once I ordered an iced chai tea latte—and record the music tracks for two songs, including the one he'd written about me that was tentatively titled "Justin."

He and Nina didn't say a word to each other. She kept her distance and let the band do their thing in the studio. I sat in the control room next to a six-foot-something handsome African American man named Boston McMurray, a music producer working for the record label that signed the Jetsetters. Boston looked like a bouncer for a nightclub. He had the deepest speaking voice I'd ever heard. He was intimidating at first, but sitting next to him I soon realized he was a gentle giant.

Nina was infatuated with the poor guy. She kept finding every excuse possible to make an appearance in the control room. She even offered to rub his shoulders because she was certain he was sore from working so hard for so many hours.

Boston liked the attention from her and flirted back. If we weren't heading to New York in the morning, I'm sure the two of them would've hooked up.

Maybe if they did, she'd be in a better mood.

At least for a while.

❖

We didn't return to the condo until after midnight. Exhaustion had set in hours ago and we were now bordering on the edges of delirium.

"Let's pack in the morning," Athena suggested, stumbling to her bedroom and closing the door.

Diego asked me to join him for a shower and I happily obliged.

"Do you really think I can do it?" he asked me as we stood face to face, mouth to mouth under a blast of warm water. "I don't think I'm a very good singer."

"You're amazing," I told him. "Everyone will love you."

And some of them might even want to steal you away from me.

"Hey," he said, as if he could read my mind. "You know I wouldn't be able to do any of this without you."

"We both know that's not true. This is your dream, your passion. I say go for it, Diego. Make this happen for yourself. You never know. You might become a huge rock star."

"But that's just it," he said. I gestured from him to turn around so I could wash his back. "I don't care about any of that. It's all bullshit."

"Don't rule anything out, though," I said. "Everything happens for a reason. Maybe Halo leaving the band can turn into a good thing."

"I haven't made up my mind," he said, "but I'm considering it. I just don't know if I can handle the attention, Justin. It's a lot of pressure."

"This is an opportunity a lot of people would kill for," I said.

"All I need is my guitar," he said, "and you. Nothing else in this world matters."

He turned back around and soap trickled down his body. I kissed him and then whispered, "I love you, Diego Delgado."

He pulled me toward him. "I love you, too."

I reached down and wrapped my hand around his hardening cock. He laughed a little and asked, "Are you doing that to convince me?"

❖

As it turned out, Darla Madrid helped Diego make the biggest professional decision of his life. It was her presence that pushed him over to the edge, made him look up at Nina and me and the other two members of his band, and say, "I'll do it."

The flight to New York was long and awkward. Nina and Diego avoided each other as much as possible. Mary Jane was making up for lost time with obnoxious chitchat and a constant barrage of questions that found nerves to get on I didn't know I had. I contemplated slipping her one of Nina's Valiums within the first hour of the flight. Athena was drafting a long love letter to Rebel Crawford, whom she was planning to reunite with in New York. Diego sat next to me working on the lyrics to a new song. I sat in silence, trying to rid myself of the terrible homesickness plaguing me.

Once we landed, we were taken by limousine to a building of rehearsal studios not far from Times Square. I took in the incredible sights of the city through the car window. I seemed to be the only one impressed with New York. No one else seemed to care.

The driver dropped us off in front of an old cream-colored building and shouted to us, "You're on the fifth floor." While Nina was making arrangements with the driver to take our luggage to the Hilton Garden Inn on Eighth Avenue and return for us in a few hours, Diego reached for my hand and squeezed it tightly.

"Can you believe it?" I said, awed. "We're in New York City."

He grinned at my childlike wonder and kissed my cheek.

Nina stepped between us, separating our hands. "None of that here, please," she insisted. "There might be press."

Inside, the building was suffocating and overheated. I started sweating, grateful I'd been sensible enough to leave my winter coat in the limo. A rickety elevator grudgingly took us to the fifth floor. The metal doors clanked and creaked open. We stepped out of it together.

That's when we saw Darla Madrid.

I gasped at the sight of her. She was blocking our path, distorting our lines of vision with her black and white polka-dotted miniskirt and matching tube top. She was chewing on a mouthful of bubblegum that smelled like watermelon. Her dark hair was bigger than ever. She wore two silver hoop earrings that were the size of door knockers. Her lipstick was too bright and one of her false eyelashes looked crooked.

"What took you guys so long?" she whined. "It's disgusting in here. I'm melting."

Athena spoke first. "What's she doing here?"

Darla looked confused and alarmed. She even looked to me for an explanation. "You guys don't know?" she asked, sounding genuinely hurt.

Nina put an arm around Darla's bare shoulders like they were long lost friends. "Mary Jane. Diego. Athena," she said as if she was their teacher and this was roll call. "I'd like for you to meet Darla Madrid—the new lead singer of the Jetsetters."

"Oh, hell no," Mary Jane said from behind me, proving once and for all she was sober and awake. And sassier than I ever imagined.

"What's going on here?" Diego asked Nina. "We never even discussed this."

"What's there to discuss?" she shot back. "Darla's a big fan. She knows all of the words to most of the songs—except for the new ones. But she's a quick study and she's happy to be here."

"Thrilled," she deadpanned, chomping on her gum.

Athena and I both looked at Diego, pleading with him.

"It's now or never," she said to him. "This is do or die, my friend."

He let out a deep sigh. He stood in front of us as if he were assuming the role of a tour guide and was about to lead us on a journey through this steam box of an antique building.

"Nina," he began, "there's been a slight change of plans."

She raised an eyebrow and dark clouds filled her already stormy eyes. "Go on."

"Athena and Mary Jane have asked me to be the lead singer of the band."

Darla exploded. *"What?"*

"It's true," Athena confirmed.

"We'd much rather have Diego be in charge than this fake bitch," Mary Jane added, endearing herself to me more and more by the second.

Thank God the pills are gone.

Darla turned on Nina. "You brought me here for *nothing*?"

Nina ignored her like she wasn't even there. "And?" she asked Diego. "What have you decided?"

He took a breath before he answered. "I'll do it."

Nina said to Darla, "You can go now. You've served your purpose here. You're dismissed." She gave her a gentle shove in the direction of the elevator. Mary Jane politely pushed the call button on Darla's behalf.

Darla looked dazed as she stepped inside the elevator, almost catatonic. "Where am I going?" she asked.

"Bye, Darla," Mary Jane said. "We'll see you later…at the Grammys!"

Darla managed a faint smile of hope. She looked insane. "You will?"

Mary Jane nodded. "We sure will, bitch…enjoy the back row!"

The elevator doors closed.

I never saw Darla Madrid again.

❖

I was sitting in the green room on a plush leather couch, prepared to watch the Jetsetters make their national television debut. I was munching on a bowl of pretzels. My eyes were glued to a television monitor hanging from the ceiling.

Athena, who had on more makeup than I'd ever seen her wear, took her place behind the drums. A pigtailed Mary Jane strapped on her pink bass guitar. Diego was front and center, dressed in black and standing behind the microphone with a pick aimed at a string on his electric guitar.

They were ready.

The door opened. I was surprised to see Nina walk in. My eyes immediately went to her hands. She was holding a few pieces of paper and a white envelope.

"Shouldn't you be in the studio with the band?" I said. "They're about to perform."

"I'm not worried about them," she said. "I wanted to take this opportunity to have a little chat with you."

She gestured to a metal table with four black plastic chairs around it. I took my cue, left my comfortable spot on the couch, and sat where she indicated I should.

"What's this about, Nina?" I asked.

"Protection," she replied.

"From?" I prompted.

"From the public," she continued, still cryptic.

She sat down across from me and slid the papers and the envelope in my direction. "I want you to sign this," she said.

"What is it?"

"It's an agreement of sorts."

"What am I agreeing to?" I asked.

"To walk away. To never see Diego again. In exchange, there's a check in the envelope made out to you for one hundred thousand dollars. To help you with…getting over him."

I glared at her. "Are you out of your fucking mind?"

"Diego's sexuality is not something the public needs to know about."

"Says who? You or Diego?"

"Actually," she said, "this is the record label's decision. They feel it's for the best."

I stood up. "Well, they can go fuck themselves and so can you."

She grabbed the sleeve of my black hoodie and stopped me. "This is a one-time offer," she explained. "The money goes away after tonight. And so do you. Whether you sign the piece of paper or not. The free ride stops here, Justin."

I struggled to not hit her. I wanted to throttle her. I wanted to call her every filthy name I could think of—and all of them were racing through my head.

Instead, I reached across her for the envelope on the table. I pulled the check out of it. I caught a glance of my name and a bunch of zeros. I ripped the check to shreds and the pieces floated down into Nina's lap.

"You have my answer," I said. "Have I made myself clear?"

I turned away from her. On the monitor screen, Diego looked directly into the camera and said, "This one goes out to my favorite barista. The true love of my life."

The Jetsetters launched into their high energy cover of the Yardbirds' classic hit "For Your Love." Ironically, it was one of the first songs I'd ever heard them play only two months ago in that little club in Chicago, when they were still Broken Corners. When Halo was still Brenda Stone. Before Diego and I had fallen in love.

Before everything changed.

❖

Nina was winning the battle she'd waged against me. She'd declared war on me almost from the beginning, from the first moment she'd spotted me in Diego's arms in the alley behind the 8-Track. She clearly saw me as some sort of threat. My very existence jeopardized the windfall she'd collect from the inevitable success of the band.

It was obvious that Nina wanted to keep Diego's private life a secret from the unknowing public eye. In order to do so, she wanted to permanently remove me from his world.

The concept seemed absurd to me. It would be impossible to hide the truth. It was misleading. It was dishonest. It was deceitful. Would fans not buy their music just because Diego was gay?

Who in the hell cares who Diego's in love with? He's a musician. Our relationship has no effect on his ability to play the guitar and write a brilliant song.

Yet Nina's words had gotten to me. They'd crawled beneath my skin and were coating my brain with doubt and fear. I would never admit it to her, but somehow Nina had manipulated me into second-guessing my role in Diego's life.

I convinced myself that Nina was right: that Diego would be better off without me.

I loved him more than anything or anyone in the world. Just the sight of him, the sound of his voice, the smell of his skin, his touch—everything about him had come to define the meaning of love to me.

I didn't doubt our love, I doubted myself. I would never truly fit into Diego's rock 'n' roll world. He was sexy and cool and wild. I was a boring guy who wanted a simple life. The two worlds would never mesh. Our future was doomed. I needed to get out before it was too late.

I didn't want to become Diego's biggest regret. I didn't want to hold him back from fame and success.

I knew I had no other choice. Just like Halo, I had to walk away.

❖

I watched Diego sleep for at least an hour before I slipped out of bed.

He stirred. He reached for me. His arm brushed across the empty space I'd left beside him.

"I'm going to get some ice," I said quietly, with the ice bucket tucked under my arm like a prop.

I was dressed. Ready to go. I'd even taken my suitcase downstairs an hour ago while Diego was in the shower. The man at the front desk promised he'd keep it safe for me.

Diego fell back into a deep sleep. I knew he wouldn't hear me, but I said the words anyway. Maybe I secretly hoped he'd wake up and convince me to change my mind. Beg me to stay.

"I love you," I said from the door of our hotel room.

Only silence responded to me.

The music world had exploded within seconds after the Jetsetters appeared on the late-night talk show. Their television debut was a smashing success. Everyone wanted to know who they were, where they'd come from, how they could get a piece of them. Nina's phone hadn't stopped ringing. I imagined she was still on her cell in her hotel room, scheming and planning and negotiating. Diego was now a famous rock star, whether he wanted to be or not.

I didn't leave because I was homesick and I wanted to go back to Chicago. I walked out of the hotel room that night because of what Nina had said to me. I left because I knew I had to give Diego his freedom. I didn't want to become his burden, his dark secret.

I waited until I was in the elevator before I started to cry.

❖

I woke Starsky up when I called her from a pay phone at JFK airport.

"Hello?" she said. The sound of her voice made me ache. I wiped my eyes.

"I'm so sorry for calling you so late," I said.

"Justin?" she said. "Is that you? Where are you? Hutch and I miss you. It's not the same without you."

"I miss you guys, too."

"I have so much to tell you," she said.

"Me too."

"Sheila broke up with me. I'm single again," she said. "But I think I like it this time."

"That's great," I said. "More time for you."

"Hey," she said, "that internship lady from your school keeps calling the shop looking for you. She said you got the position you wanted at the advertising agency."

I closed my eyes and said a silent prayer of gratitude. "Are you serious?"

"Yeah. She said you start in January," Starsky explained. "So I guess I'm losing you forever, then."

"No," I said, my voice quivering. "Actually, I'm coming back to Chicago."

"You are?" I could hear the happiness in Starsky's voice. It made me smile. It made me feel like everything was going to be okay.

"Yes," I told her. "I'm coming home."

CHAPTER TWENTY-THREE

Diego made every possible attempt to contact me. Letters. Postcards. E-mails. Voice-mail messages begging me to call him back. I could hear the horrible ache in his words, breaking my heart each time I heard his voice. Soon, I forced myself to stop reading his letters. I deleted the messages he left without listening to them. I changed my phone number and e-mail address. I became unreachable. Invisible.

Then he stopped trying.

I retreated to the solace of my apartment for a few days, allowing the reality to sink in. Diego and I were over. Never again would we be together. Wasn't that what I wanted?

Then why do I feel so incredibly sad?

Within months, the Jetsetters became rock royalty. They released three back-to-back hit singles, propelling them into stardom. Their debut album sold in the millions. Their world tour filled arenas. Their trend-setting music videos brought them artistic acclaim. More awards were bestowed on them than I could count.

For a while, I followed the band's every move, nearly obsessing over their interviews and television appearances. But when I started to see the deep sorrow in Diego's eyes, the damage I'd caused became all too real. I'd shattered his heart into a million pieces. He was a broken man. It was evident in every word he spoke and sang. He'd given up on everything. I blamed myself for the constant state of misery he appeared to be living in.

The guilt became nearly impossible for me to deal with. I agonized over my decision for months, wondering what would've happened if I'd stayed.

If I would've been brave enough to love Diego. Like I'd promised him I always would.

To move on with my life, I tried my best to forget. I wanted to purge every memory of Diego from my mind. To do so, I kept myself busy as much as possible. School. Work. Television. Success.

I settled into my self-imposed lonely existence, knowing damn well with each day that passed that I'd made the worst decision of my life.

❖

A year later, Geoffrey Cole landed his own national radio show. His first guest was Rebel Crawford. She had a huge hit single with a slowed-down cover version of the Missing Persons '80s new-wave classic "Walking in L.A."

I hadn't heard from Diego. Or Athena. Or Mary Jane.

Not that I was really expecting to.

I tuned in and listened to Geoffrey's show, out of curiosity.

Geoffrey spoke first. "Rebel Crawford, you came out of nowhere. How did you get started?"

She let out a long, melodramatic sigh. "The hard way, Geoffrey. In coffee shops. In Santa Monica," she said. "You know, I used to date Athena Parker."

"Who?" he asked.

She giggled and said, "Exactly. She's the drummer for the Jetsetters. But all the world cares about is Diego Delgado. He's everywhere."

"Athena Parker," he repeated. "Didn't she date Veronica Marie for a while also, before that big Internet scandal?"

"I have no idea how *that* happened," Rebel said, feigning innocence. "What a shame for poor Veronica Marie. Anyway, back to me. So I dated her for a while. I got into the scene and I loved it. I knew I had to be big."

"Let's talk about your CD."

You could hear the smug smile in her voice. "It's called *Let's Just Be Me*. I wrote all of the songs on it. We're touring with a band called Havoc. Do you know Vicki Sheppard? She's the lead singer. Aren't you married to her ex-best friend?"

The disdain in Geoffrey's voice was thick. "You mean… Darla Madrid?"

"Yeah…*her*," Rebel sneered.

Geoffrey's tone was one of disgust. "She's a…singer."

"She's a pop tart," Rebel countered. "Anyway, we're on tour. Come see us."

"Do you perform with Havoc?"

"No, I have my own band. But Havoc will be big."

"You think so?"

"I know so," she said. "I have good instinct. Just like you used to when you had that column and everyone read it for—"

"Well, enough about them."

"I agree," she said. "Just check out the show. I'm the wave of the future."

"I hear you fired your manager."

"Nina Grey?" she said. "Yeah, I told her she needed to dry out for a while. She was throwing back too many cocktails at my expense. Last I heard she was living on some sheep ranch in Montana."

"Montana? Are you sure about that? Someone told me she bought the Geneva Recording Studios and is personally handling all aspects of Diego Delgado's career."

"Yeah, yeah, yeah," she said. "By the way, I'm dating

Boston McMurray. He isn't very bright and I keep him around for the sake of eye candy, but he adores me," she said. "Just like everyone else in this world."

"You're quite…humble…aren't you?" Geoffrey asked.

"Um, no," she said. "Not really. So…before I congratulate you and Darla Madrid on your dysfunctional marriage and your dramatic divorce and her short-lived career, I'd like to offer this piece of advice to your listeners, Geoffrey," Rebel said. She took a breath before finishing the interview with: "Nobody walks in L.A."

❖

I found Halo by accident. I was in Santa Monica on a business trip, helping a hard-to-please client launch a new ad campaign. By the fifth night, the walls of my hotel room felt like they were closing in on me. I needed some air.

I strolled down the Third Street Promenade, stopping to listen to the street musicians I discovered along the way. I made my way over to the Santa Monica Pier, relishing the calming sound of the Pacific Ocean and breathing in the invigorating salty air. Immediately, I flashed back to the moment Diego and I had shared standing in the shadow of Navy Pier in Chicago. I wondered if I'd ever see him again. If I did, what would I say? How could I ever repair the destruction I'd caused?

My stomach grumbled, reminding me I hadn't eaten all day. I searched for an open coffee shop or an all-night diner. Not far from the beach, I spotted a golden neon sign twinkling and flashing the word "Pancakes." I stepped inside the retro-style restaurant and immediately felt a sense of comfort. There was a down-home appeal to the place. It was simple and cozy.

I slid into an empty booth and scanned the menu.

Then I heard the voice. I looked up. I breathed deep.

"I don't believe it," she said. "What in the hell are you doing here, lover boy?"

"Oh my God," I heard myself say. "Halo?"

She shook her head and tapped the edge of her pink-and-white name tag. "I'm Brenda," she said. "I've always been Brenda."

She looked exactly the same: the sexy smile, the wild hair, the not-so-subtle provocativeness. The only difference was the polyester pink-and-white waitress uniform she was wearing. She looked like she'd stepped out of a classic episode of the TV series *Alice*.

She glanced down at the empty side of the booth across from me. "May I?" she asked.

"Of course," I said.

"You look like hell, Justin. What happened to you?"

I didn't know how to answer her question. Was my heartache that apparent? I shrugged and mumbled, "I don't sleep much."

"How long has it been?" she asked. "Since I last saw you?"

"Just a little over five years," I answered fast. I worried she'd assume I'd been counting each second that had passed since, so I quickly added, "I think."

"I heard you left him," she said. She folded her arms across her chest and gave me that interrogating stare of hers. "What the fuck happened to you two?"

"Nina…" I began. "She told me…"

Brenda held up a hand. "Say no more."

"I haven't spoken to him," I explained.

"Neither have I," she said. "To any of them. I miss those fuckers."

"I heard the band broke up."

She nodded. "The Jetsetters are dead. They've all moved on."

"Where is everyone?" I asked.

"Do you mean Diego?" she shot back. "He's teaching inner-city kids how to play guitar, from what I hear. He started a school of some sort. He hides from the press the best he can.

He always hated that. He never wanted to be famous." I nodded, remembering. "And he's single, in case you're interested. He always has been."

"I don't think he'll ever want to see me again," I said.

We locked eyes. "You sure about that?" she asked. "We both know you were the best thing that ever happened to him."

I felt the tears rising. "Don't say that to me," I said. "Please."

"It's the truth," she said. "Otherwise it wouldn't hurt like hell."

"You have no idea…" I stammered.

"You're wrong," she said. "He'll never be the same without you. We both know that."

I wiped my eyes with the back of my hand. "Is everyone okay? Mary Jane? Athena?"

"Athena started another band. Some all-girl punk project."

"Oh," I said. "I hadn't heard."

"Mary Jane teaches yoga and lives in Santa Barbara," she explained. "The fucking nut is a hippie vegan now and chants like a bad habit."

"Have you been here this whole time?" I asked. I glanced around the restaurant. "Working here?"

She grinned. I realized in that second how much I'd missed her. "Don't let the uniform fool you, lover boy. I own the place," she said. "So, whatever you're eating…it's on the house."

"You don't have to do that," I said. "You don't owe me anything, Brenda."

"Yeah, I do," she said. I gave her a look. I was confused. What had I ever done for her? Put up with her crazy, drunken antics? "You were there for me, Justin. And I don't know if I ever thanked you for that."

I closed the menu, ready to order. "It looks like you made a great decision," I said. "To walk away from it all. To live the life you really wanted."

Brenda stood up. She looked down at me. I tried to decode the strange expression in her eyes. It was a bittersweet mixture of happiness and sorrow.

"I've never been happier," she said to me. "What about you?"

CHAPTER TWENTY-FOUR

My heart began to race as the cab driver turned onto Sunset Boulevard.

"Geneva Recording Studios, you said?" the old man asked.

My mouth felt dry from the three martinis I'd consumed in the airport bar just minutes before. It hurt my throat to speak, but I did. "Yes. I think we're close, actually."

The cab pulled up in front of the nondescript bungalow-style building a few minutes later. I leaned forward and handed the driver a fifty. "Will you wait for me?"

"It'll cost you," he said.

I breathed deep and replied, "It already has."

I opened the door and stepped out of the cab. Sunset Boulevard was an intoxicating daze of lights and billboards. I felt dizzy. I glanced up to the hovering palm trees and gathered my courage. I moved to the building, to the glass door.

I entered the recording studio, gripping the shoulder strap of my computer bag for dear life. The wood-paneled claustrophobic lobby was deserted. I heard music coming from farther down the hallway. I moved in the direction the jazzy piano music was coming from. I'd only taken a few steps when my path was suddenly blocked. Nina stepped into the hallway from an office of some type. Her nose was different but her hair was still frosted blond, just longer. She looked older, as to be expected, but her steel gray eyes still burned with an evil glare. She recognized me at once. It was as if she were expecting me.

"What do *you* want?" she asked.

"Is he here?"

She gave me a hard look and sighed. "Why now, Justin?" she asked. "After all these fucking years? It was just an affair, for God's sake."

My voice rose. "Is he here?!" I demanded.

Nina looked startled by my display of aggression, my urgency. "No."

I took a step toward her. "Are you lying to me?"

"Why would I?"

"Tell me where he is, Nina."

She shrugged. "How should I know?"

"Tell me, damn it." I struggled to maintain my composure. I looked her directly in the eyes and said, "You owe it to me."

She held my stare for a moment before answering. "He's in Santa Monica. Try the pier. He likes to hang out there when he's working on new lyrics."

I turned. I headed toward the exit.

Behind me, Nina's words hit the back of my head as she yelled, "Don't fuck things up for him again! He's making a comeback!"

I tore out of the recording studio with a vengeance. I couldn't get to the cab fast enough.

❖

The ocean air felt like a much-needed hug wrapping around my body. I walked down the pier through the pools of multicolored lights cast on the ground by the massive Ferris wheel hovering above the passing crowds. I moved through the sea of strangers, searching. In the distance, the reflective surface of the moonlit Pacific Ocean seemed like a beacon of hope. It urged me on.

Then I heard the guitar, the music: Bob Dylan's distinctive

lyrics from "I Want You," sung in a voice that had haunted me for the last twelve years.

I saw Diego. He was sitting on a bench, facing the water, the horizon. His eyes were lifted toward the moon as if he were singing directly to it. He was a little heavier, older, but still possessed that irresistible rebellious charm. I approached him from the side. The music suddenly stopped, as if Diego sensed my presence without even setting eyes on me.

Then he turned.

He blinked a few times. He breathed in deep. "Justin?" he said. "My God, where have you been?"

My thoughts were moving quicker than my mouth. "I was at the airport," stumbled out of my lips. "I came to find you."

Diego stood up, still clutching his guitar. "Why?"

"Because…I wanted to see you," I said. "I had to see you, Diego."

Diego lowered his head. He sounded broken when he spoke. "You just left."

I moved slow, cautious. I sat down on the bench. "I know," I said. "And I'm sorry. And I'd like to explain to you why."

Diego turned. He looked down into my eyes. "You never came back for me. I was scared. Nina said—"

I reached out. I took Diego's hand into mine. I brought him back down to the bench to be next to me. "I want you to forgive me," I said.

Diego's eyes swelled with tears. The emotion surprised me. "How could you leave?" he asked.

I slipped an arm around him. "It was the biggest regret of my life. I convinced myself that you'd be better off without me. I didn't want to stand in the way."

Our eyes met. "You were everything to me," he said. "You still are."

"Even after…all this time?"

He nodded. "I knew we'd find each other again," he said. "When the time was right."

"Is it?" I asked, trying to hide the hope in my voice. "Is it the right time, Diego?"

He looked away. "Things got really fucked up for me."

"I know," I said. "I read all about it."

Diego's jaw tightened. "A has-been. That's what they call me."

I moved closer to him. "I think you're brilliant."

Diego almost smiled. "You like the music?"

I nodded. "I own every CD."

"Then you heard the song? The one I wrote about you."

"I know it well."

Diego wiped his eyes with the back of his sleeve. "The record label—they made me change the name of it to 'Justine.' It wasn't my idea."

I squeezed my grip on Diego's hand. "It sounds like people have been making decisions for you for a long time."

Diego thought about it for a moment and then, he agreed. "Yeah, they have."

I touched Diego's face, pressed an index finger against his lips. I looked deep into his tear-filled cinnamon eyes and said, "Maybe it's time you make one for yourself."

Diego titled his head then, rested it on my shoulder. "Like what?"

"Let's start with coffee," I said. "Would you let me buy you a cup?"

He kissed my cheek and said, "I would really like that."

"Great," I said. "I know the perfect place."

I started to stand up but Diego stopped me. "Let's go in a minute," he suggested. "For now, I just want to be right beside you."

"Okay," I agreed.

"We can sit here," he said. "We can look at the water. The moon. Each other."

The words came from my heart. "I love you, Diego."

He placed his guitar on his knee and positioned himself,

ready to play. “I love you, too,” he said. “I’d like to play a song for you, Justin. I really think you’ll like it. I wrote it just this morning. It’s about you. It’s about us.” He looked into my eyes and whispered, “It’s a love song.”

About the Author

David-Matthew Barnes is the award-winning author of the novels *Mesmerized*, *Accidents Never Happen*, *Swimming to Chicago*, *The Jetsetters*, and *Wonderland* (forthcoming, 2013). He wrote and directed the coming-of-age film *Frozen Stars*, which received worldwide distribution. He is the author of over forty stage plays that have been performed in three languages in eight countries. His literary work has appeared in over one hundred publications including *The Best Stage Scenes*, *The Best Men's Stage Monologues*, *The Best Women's Stage Monologues*, *The Comstock Review*, *Review Americana*, and *The Southeast Review*. Barnes is the recipient of the Hart Crane Memorial Poetry Award. In addition, he's received the Carrie McCray Literary Award and the Slam Boston Award for Best Play, and has earned double awards for poetry and playwriting in the World AIDS Day Writing Contest. He is a member of the Dramatists Guild of America. Barnes earned a Master of Fine Arts in creative writing at Queens University of Charlotte in North Carolina. Barnes is a faculty member at Southern Crescent Technical College in Griffin, Georgia, where he teaches courses in humanities and theatre.

Books Available From Bold Strokes Books

Month of Sundays by Yolanda Wallace. Love doesn't always happen overnight; sometimes it takes a month of Sundays. (978-1-60282-739-4)

Jacob's War by C.P. Rowlands. ATF Special Agent Allison Jacob's task force is in the middle of an all-out war, from the streets to the boardrooms of America. Small business owner Katie Blackburn is the latest victim who accidentally breaks it wide open, but she may break AJ's heart at the same time. (978-1-60282-740-0)

The Pyramid Waltz by Barbara Ann Wright. Princess Katya Nar Umbriel wants a perfect romance, but her Fiendish nature and duties to the crown mean she can never tell the truth—until she meets Starbride, a woman who gets to the heart of every secret, even if it will be the death of her. (978-1-60282-741-7)

The Secret of Othello by Sam Cameron. Florida teen detectives Steven and Denny risk their lives to search for a sunken NASA satellite-but under the waves, no one can hear you scream… (978-1-60282-742-4)

Andy Squared by Jennifer Lavoie. Andrew never thought anyone could come between him and his twin sister, Andrea…until Ryder rode into town. (978-1-60282-743-1)

Finding Bluefield by Elan Barnehama. Set in the backdrop of Virginia and New York and spanning the years 1960–1982, *Finding Bluefield* chronicles the lives of Nicky Stewart, Barbara Philips, and their son, Paul, as they struggle to define themselves as a family. (978-1-60282-744-8)

The Jettsetters by David-Matthew Barnes. As rock band the Jetsetters skyrocket from obscurity to superstardom, Justin Holt, a lonely barista, and Diego Delgado, the band's guitarist, fight with everything they have to stay together, despite the chaos and fame. (978-1-60282-745-5)

Strange Bedfellows by Rob Byrnes. Partners in life and crime, Grant Lambert and Chase LaMarca are hired to make a politician's compromising photo disappear, but what should be an easy job quickly spins out of control. (978-1-60282-746-2)

Dreaming of Her by Maggie Morton. Isa has begun to dream of the most amazing woman—a woman named Lilith with a gorgeous face, an amazing body, and the ability to turn Isa on like no other. But Lilith is just a dream...isn't she? (978-1-60282-847-6)

Speed Demons by Gun Brooke. When NASCAR star Evangeline Marshall returns to the race track after a close brush with death, will famous photographer Blythe Pierce document her triumph and reciprocate her love—or will they succumb to their respective demons and fail? (978-1-60282-678-6)

Summoning Shadows: A Rosso Lussuria Vampire Novel by Winter Pennington. The Rosso Lussuria vampires face enemies both old and new, and to prevail they must call on even more strange alliances, unite as a clan, and draw on every weapon within their reach—but with a clan of vampires, that's easier said than done. (978-1-60282-679-3)

Sometime Yesterday by Yvonne Heidt. When Natalie Chambers learns her Victorian house is haunted by a pair of lovers and a Dark Man, can she and her lover Van Easton solve the mystery that will set the ghosts free and banish the evil presence in the house? Or will they have to run to survive as well? (978-1-60282-680-9)

Into the Flames by Mel Bossa. In order to save one of his patients, psychiatrist Jamie Scarborough will have to confront his own monsters—including those he unknowingly helped create. (978-1-60282-681-6)

Coming Attractions: Author's Edition by Bobbi Marolt. For Helen Townsend, chasing turns to caring, and caring turns to loving, but will love take five steps back and turn to leaving? (978-1-60282-732-5)

OMGqueer, edited by Radclyffe and Katherine E. Lynch. Through stories imagined and told by youth across America, this anthology provides a snapshot of queerness at the dawn of the new millennium. (978-1-60282-682-3)

Oath of Honor by Radclyffe. A First Responders novel. First do no harm…First Physician of the United States Wes Masters discovers that being the president's doctor demands more than brains and personal sacrifice—especially when politics is the order of the day. (978-1-60282-671-7)

A Question of Ghosts by Cate Culpepper. Becca Healy hopes Dr. Joanne Call can help her learn if her mother really committed suicide—but she's not sure she can handle her mother's ghost, a decades-old mystery, and lusting after the difficult Dr. Call without some serious chocolate consumption. (978-1-60282-672-4)

The Night Off by Meghan O'Brien. When Emily Parker pays for a taboo role-playing fantasy encounter from the Xtreme Scenarios escort agency, she expects to surrender control—but never imagines losing her heart to dangerous butch Nat Swayne. (978-1-60282-673-1)

Sara by Greg Herren. A mysterious and beautiful new student at Southern Heights High School stirs things up when students start dying. (978-1-60282-674-8)

Fontana by Joshua Martino. Fame, obsession, and vengeance collide in a novel that asks: What if America's greatest hero was gay? (978-1-60282-675-5)

Lemon Reef by Robin Silverman. What would you risk for the memory of your first love? When Jenna Ross learns her high school love Del Soto died on Lemon Reef, she refuses to accept the medical examiner's report of a death from natural causes and risks everything to find the truth. (978-1-60282-676-2)

The Dirty Diner: Gay Erotica on the Menu, edited by Jerry L. Wheeler. Gay erotica set in restaurants, featuring food, sex, and men—could you really ask for anything more? (978-1-60282-677-9)

Sweat: Gay Jock Erotica by Todd Gregory. Sizzling tales of smoking-hot sex with the athletic studs everyone fantasizes about. (978-1-60282-669-4)

The Marrying Kind by Ken O'Neill. Just when successful wedding planner Adam More decides to protest inequality by quitting the business and boycotting marriage entirely, his only sibling announces her engagement. (978-1-60282-670-0)

Missing by P.J. Trebelhorn. FBI agent Olivia Andrews knows exactly what she wants out of life, but then she's forced to rethink everything when she meets fellow agent Sophie Kane while investigating a child abduction. (978-1-60282-668-7)